SPARK

BURNING MOON ~ BOOK ONE

R.K. CLOSE

BIG TREE PUBLISHING

BURNING MOON SERIES

❀ Created with Vellum

NOVELS BY R.K. CLOSE

Vampire Files Trilogy

RED NIGHT

RED MOON

RED DREAM

RED DAWN

COMING 2020

BURNING MOON SERIES

SPARK

IGNITE

BLAZE

COMING 2020

ASHES

$\mathcal{L}$iam

The night was for hunting.

The sound of dried leaves crunching beneath small animals as they scurry to find shelter after catching my scent competed with the sound of crickets chirping their night song.

Light from the moon bathed the forest in cool blue shades. At night the temperature would dip below freezing, but that never concerned me. I always ran hot.

A certain smell filled my nostrils. This was what I'd been seeking—the hunt was on. It made me feel more alive than anything in my human existence ever had.

My heart pounded fast and hard, and I felt as if the sound could be heard by every creature for miles around. Four strong legs drove me forward, closer to the prey—our prey. But it is mine first. I was alpha.

Soon, I could hear another heartbeat racing faster than my own. Even the fallen branches and twigs cracking under my paws couldn't drown out the panicked thumping of the deer's heart as it made a desperate effort to flee.

Finally, the moment came. I leaped, making one final contact with a fallen tree to propel my body into the air. I collided with the deer, causing the frightened animal to miss a crucial step that sent it crashing to the ground. I was on it before it could recover. Sharp teeth sank deep into the animal's flesh—my teeth.

EARLY MORNING LIGHT WOKE ME. That, and the feeling of sharp objects poking into my backside. The sun had not risen over the mountains yet, and I could see my breath as it formed, passing clouds in front of my face. Even though my body temperature ran hotter than an ordinary human, I had begun to shiver. *Being naked hadn't helped.*

I stood and brushed off the leaves and pine needles that clung to my damp body. Scanning the surrounding woods, I searched for my brothers. When I didn't see them, I started the cold walk toward the place we'd stashed our clothing the evening before.

Something about discovering I was a wolf-shifter freed me of modesty I'd once had. I'd been caught naked before, but fortunately, it wasn't by any of the locals. I always figured we could have confessed to being nudists if we'd had to. While the notion was odd, it wouldn't have been unforgivable.

The good people of Flagstaff might actually accept that concept over the idea of werewolves living among them. Especially, being so close to the town of Sedona. That town had nudist, spiritualist, and a few self-proclaimed witches.

I heard one of my brothers long before I saw him emerge from the forest. Some of the benefits of being a shifter—heightened strength, speed, and hearing.

Seth fell into step beside me, and we walked in silence, attempting to shake off the deep sleep that followed shifting forms.

We reached the small cave—it wasn't large enough to crawl more than three or four feet inside—and pulled out three bundles of clothing and personal items. The freezing temperature was an excellent motivation for dressing quickly.

When I had my jeans and flannel shirt on, I sat on a fallen log to pull on my hiking boots. Seth still hadn't bothered to button his shirt or zip his pants. Instead, he'd checked his phone, like it wasn't freezing, or he had no sense of urgency.

Only a few minutes had passed before Cole came running toward us *in all his naked glory.* Cole, my youngest brother, always had a ton of energy and struggled with slow and easy. The look on his face warned me that it wasn't just his usual enthusiasm for life. Something was wrong.

"We got trouble," Cole said, as he reached us and took the pile of clothes Seth handed him.

Cole was shorter and stockier than Seth and me. His sandy blond hair was short on the sides but a bit longer on top. When he was younger, it used to hang over his eyes, and he was forever combing it back with his fingers.

"What's wrong?" Seth asked. I scanned the forest, alert to any signs of trouble.

"I stumbled across two dead campers about a mile back up the trail." Cole looked shook up, but finding dead people could do that to a person. Cole was also a firefighter and EMT, like Seth and me.

"Did you…" Seth started to ask.

Cole looked confused for a second until he realized what Seth was implying, then he looked indignant. "No. Of course not. It wasn't me. I just found them."

Seth and I exchanged a glance. We all knew that we only retained flashes of memory while in wolf form. It was the fear of hurting someone that sent us far into the mountains when we needed to shift. It was an itch that had to be scratched. I'd taken a life once, but I tried not to think about that if I could help it.

Cole dressed more quickly than Seth or I had, and was soon leading us to where he'd found the bodies.

"How'd they die?" I asked as we made our way through the woods.

"I can't be sure. I didn't do more than check for a pulse, even though I knew they were gone. Figured since I'm a fire-fighter the police would wonder why I didn't check. There's also something else odd about it." Cole glanced sideways at me.

"What?" I asked.

"You'll have to see for yourself. Or smell," Cole mumbled, before turning his attention ahead. He didn't speak again until we saw a red tent in the distance. "That's it."

We were about a hundred yards away from the campsite, but that was close enough for me to know what Cole was talking about. There was the smell of death, but not just the campers. There was something else.

"What the hell is that?" I asked as we drew closer.

"It's not that bad," Seth said. "Nothing I've ever smelled before, though."

Cole and I stopped to gawk at Seth. "Not that bad?" Cole asked. "That smell is not right. No way."

"It's different, that's all. I don't know what you *girls* are getting your panties in a wad over," Seth defended.

I had a bad feeling about the smell, but I kept it to myself. We reached the edge of the camp, and I took in the scene before me. A small camp table was knocked over on its side, and a few items were strewn across the ground. The tent seemed to be intact. "Did you check for anyone else?" I asked.

"Yes, I used a stick to pull the tent flap back, and then searched the perimeter. Nothing."

I nodded and walked carefully to the first body. It was a

young woman, mid to late twenties, with long brown hair. She wore a blue down coat, and a beanie of the same color was lying a few feet away. Her eyes stared blankly at the morning sky, while her long brown hair was strewn all around her and partially across her face.

"Look at her neck," Cole said.

I carefully moved the strands of hair away. There was some dried blood on her neck, but only two bruised puncture wounds could be seen. I did notice that the front of her jacket looked as though it had been sliced up, but there was no blood or obvious injury. Possibly someone grabbed her by the coat. The location of the tears would support that theory, but who has the strength to put their fingers through nylon like that?

"What could that smell be, Liam?" Cole asked.

I glanced at the male a few feet away. By the angle of his arm, it had been broken before he died. He also had a wound on his throat, but the damage was more evident than the woman.

It seemed to me that they died, most likely, six or seven hours ago. It bothered me that they died in the same proximity my brothers and I was. Something other than us was hunting last night.

The Coconino National Forest was 1.8 million acres of territory, but this particular patch of woods was ours. We chose it because of its remote location and the fact that people rarely used this part of the mountain range. These unlucky folks were way off the grid, but occasionally people wanted to be away from it all.

I spotted a book of matches next to the tent and bent to pick it up. After dusting it off, I handed it to Seth. He turned it over in his fingers and then passed it to Cole.

"The Burning Moon Bar," Cole read, then looked up at me. "They must have been in town at some point. Look at their gear. This was carried in from a car. That means their vehicle must be in the same parking area as ours was."

Seth gives me a grim look. "We should walk away, right?"

I shook my head. "I don't believe we can. Think about it. We were roaming all over these woods last night. If we don't report this, we could find the finger pointing at us. Whoever or whatever did this isn't a shifter, but they aren't human either. The safest thing to do is report it. I'll say that we came across the bodies and then hiked back to the truck for better cell service."

I looked at them, and they nodded. This wasn't the situation I had in mind, but it was the reason I kept our camping gear in the truck so we could support the well-known belief that we camped together often.

I held out my hand, and Cole passed me the matchbook case, which I slipped into my pocket, then headed for the parking lot. Cole and Seth followed.

Ordinarily, we'd be laughing and cutting up by now, but this morning was somber and gray, matching our moods and out of respect for the two people whose lives were cut short.

When we reached the clearing that passed for a trailhead parking lot, I found a small blue car with two dangling hearts hanging from the rearview mirror. The vehicle had California plates, most likely they were tourists passing through, or college students attending Northern Arizona University.

They must have arrived sometime after us the evening before. I made the call that would bring the sheriff and open a can of worms I wished we could avoid. Whatever did this, I hoped it had already left town, even though I was curious about what else was out there, besides shifters like us. Not that we needed any mysteries to solve. Our own past was full of unanswered questions.

A plethora of people continued to arrive, crowding the small dirt parking lot. Each new arrival seemed to stretch my nerves even tighter. The sheriff was first to come, followed by, most likely, every deputy in town. The crime scene crew showed up and headed into the woods, dressed in white jumpers covering their regular clothing, and carrying boxes that held their supplies and cameras.

When the coroner arrived, I'd hoped that would be the end of the show. Seth, Cole, and I had sorted out our stories before anyone arrived. I knew it was standard procedure for the sheriff to question witnesses individually, even if the sheriff had known us personally for years.

The sheriff's office worked alongside the fire department on many scenes, so we were on a first name basis with many of the deputies, which helped to validate our story. We were known as avid campers and hikers who enjoyed spending time outdoors, so our reason for being on the mountain wasn't suspicious. The sheriff seemed to accept our explanation without issue.

Cole, Seth, and I stood around my truck and watched the

comings and goings of people who had been called out to do their grim jobs. There was an unhealthy level of excitement that I didn't appreciate. Two young people had died for no good reason...most likely by something unnatural.

Unnatural. What did that say about us, I wondered?

"I think they bought it," Seth said, under his breath.

I nodded. We needed to get back to town soon. Other firefighters had been called to cover our shifts until we could return. It wasn't that bad since the firefighters would receive extra pay for the inconvenience and they wouldn't have to work an entire twenty-four-hour shift, but it was a great excuse to leave as soon as possible.

My brothers and I were lucky. The fire department policy didn't allow family members to run on the same crew, but since it was a small town, they had turned a blind eye when I pulled Seth and then later, Cole onto my shift. It wasn't like the department had officially granted permission, but they hadn't brought it up with me in over a year.

I was beginning to think we'd make it out of this unscathed when the news van pulled into the crowded parking lot. That was the last thing we needed.

"Don't speak to any reporters. We're under no obligation to be interviewed by any of the news stations," I said quietly.

"Won't they be suspicious?" Cole asked, glancing over at the van.

"No, plenty of people are camera shy. We don't need an excuse. They don't have a right to interview us. Just stick to your guns and don't give in. Hopefully, they won't bother."

Seth whistled, and I turned to follow his gaze. Two women had just climbed out of the van. One was getting equipment out of the back. She wore jeans, sneakers, and a flannel jacket. She had curly dark hair and a friendly face.

But it was the other woman who made my gut clench and my heart pound in my ears. I could feel the the perspiration on my neck and forehead. Her long blonde hair shone like a halo of gold in an otherwise colorless scene. She wore a straight tight sirt, and a matching blazer that didn't look warm enough for the weather.

My reaction to the pretty blonde reporter was immediate and powerful. I was a man, I'd always appreciated an attractive woman, but my response to her was over the top. I wondered why? I tried to hide my discomfort from my brothers.

She was checking her face in the side mirror of the van—not a good sign. She was planning to report the news on camera.

"Damn it," I said turning away.

"Nice," Seth said, drawing out the word. "Are you sure we can't do an interview?"

"She's pretty hot, if you ask me," Cole volunteered.

"I didn't," I barked.

My brother's infatuation with the woman was grating on my last nerve. Someone like her could expose us, or so I told myself.

"I've seen her on the news. She's feisty, just like I like 'em," Seth said, watching her interview the sheriff.

"Stay away from her," I growled. Both Cole and Seth turned to gape at me.

I hadn't meant for it to come out like that. The situation had me on edge.

"Easy there, big brother. I won't play in your sandbox. All you had to do was say you liked her," Seth teased.

"I don't like her. I don't even know her. She could cause a lot of trouble for us. Don't do anything stupid, like date her," I said, trying to cover my initial reaction. It had caught me off guard, and I glanced over at the reporter again.

Seth and Cole exchanged smug glances before turning their knowing gazes back on me.

"Sure, Liam. Anything you say," Seth taunted.

I rolled my eyes and shook my head at his suggestion that I was interested in the curvy blonde. It was nerves, nothing more.

"I thought you were going to bite my head off." Seth chuckled, and Cole grinned. I ignored them and looked away just in time to see the sheriff pointing us out to the reporter.

"Here she comes," Cole said under his breath.

"Get into the truck," I ordered. "Now," I said when they hesitated.

"Damn, Liam. You're always a buzz-kill," Seth grumbled, before heading for the truck. Cole followed him. They both threw curious glances over their shoulder as they went.

Turning, I faced the woman who was trying to make her way across the parking lot, nearly killing herself in those tall, pointy shoes. It was painful to watch.

Before she reached me, I yelled to the sheriff, "We're taking off. You know where to find us if you need to."

The sheriff waved, and I turned toward the truck. I caught the look of panic on her face as she realized I was leaving.

"Excuse me, Captain McKenzie?" I stopped dead in my tracks. Her voice sounded like honey, making me think of soft silk being pulled over my skin. I hadn't meant to stop. I'd meant to ignore her and drive away.

Slowly, I turned around. She was even more beautiful up close. Not the sort of typical beauty you see on the cover of magazines, but breathtaking in her own way. A sudden desire to possess her, body, mind, and soul, rushed through my awareness. *What was wrong with me?*

Her soft pale skin screamed to be touched, and I wanted to feel it. Her blonde hair hung in loose waves around her face and shoulders. Was it as soft as it looked? I shook my head, trying to chase away the images from my mind. If I believed in witches, I'd be convinced she'd cast a spell on me.

She had jogged the last few yards. Impressive—in those shoes. I was beginning to appreciate the way the heels showed off the muscular curve of her calves. Her heartbeat was fast, and I could smell desire on her. *Which meant she found me attractive as well. Damn it all to hell.*

"I'm leaving, Miss. What do you want?" My reaction to her made my words sound angry. I could tell my response caught her off guard. For the briefest moment, she looked hurt. Just as quickly she covered her initial expression with a professional smile. It was like a mask dropped into place.

I felt wrong about my behavior toward her, but I knew it was for the best.

3

*J*essica ~ The sheriff pointed out the firefighters who had found the bodies. "That's them, over there. Captain Liam McKenzie and his brothers, Seth and Cole—all firefighters with Flagstaff Fire Department."

I had enough information to know the hiker's death was not a cut and dried case, even if the sheriff refused to elaborate or speculate on the deaths. Sometimes, the things we don't say speaks volumes. If the deaths turned out to be accidental, I could have still pulled some serious screen time reporting on it.

I followed the direction he was pointing, and spotted three men standing in a huddle. They were staring at us.

"Thank you, Sheriff. I'll go speak to them." I turned toward Daisy, my camera person and friend. "Let's do this, Daisy. I want to set the shot up with the forest as the backdrop. Can you do that?" I asked.

"Can a duck quack?" Daisy said, lugging her large camera on her small shoulders. Daisy was an attractive woman with curly brown hair that was usually hidden under a baseball cap. Her best feature was her soulful eyes, also hidden behind large, round black-rimmed glasses.

I had all the details the sheriff was willing to share for now. I needed to bring in a human element to the story, so I headed straight for the brothers. It was hard to miss the purely masculine portrait the three men made. All were ruggedly handsome and seemed well built.

I walked toward them, making a mental note of their attire—jeans and flannel shirts under down coats. Typical Flagstaff clothing. I noticed they didn't wear gloves or beanies, like most of the other people on the scene. It didn't look like the cold bothered them much. They must be natives of Flagstaff.

As for me, I was struggling to keep my teeth from chattering. I was a transplant from blazing hot Phoenix, and I'd been freezing my bootie off since summer. Hard to believe Flagstaff was in the same state. I didn't even own the proper winter clothing for living here, and it had been six months already.

I watched as two of the men walked to an older model truck and got in. The other man, a tall, well-built guy with short blond hair and gorgeous blue eyes, looked right at me, then yelled to the sheriff that he was leaving.

Panicked, I jogged to catch him before he left. "Excuse me. Captain McKenzie?" I called.

The man stopped when he heard his name, but didn't turn around right away. I had begun to wonder if he'd truly heard me when he turned toward me. I almost stopped breathing when I saw his face up close. It was like I had one of those déjà vu moments that can't be explained.

But what surprised me even more was the look the captain gave me when he turned that handsome, yet hostile face my way.

Captain McKenzie glared at me like he hated me. "I'm leaving, Miss. What do you want?" he practically growled.

His acidic response caught me by surprise, because men usually had a more favorable response toward me. It made doing my job easier. *Usually.*

I corrected my face and gave him the friendliest smile I could manage. "Captain McKenzie, I'm—"

"I know who you are, and I'm not interested in being interviewed," he said, turning to leave.

I looked at Daisy in confusion. Daisy shrugged her shoulders, but motioned for me to keep trying.

I cleared my throat and trotted after him. "I know this must have been a terrible ordeal, finding the bodies, but—" I had just reached his side and impulsively placed a hand on his as he reached for the door of the truck.

A spark, much like an electrical shock, passed up my arm, and I jerked my hand back. I couldn't be sure, but it certainly seemed like Liam McKenzie felt the same thing. Surprise crossed his face for a shadow of a second, leaving his expression unguarded.

He was beautiful in an entirely male sort of way, and I felt my body flush in response. In that second, I thought I saw his eyes flash from blue to amber. It was an odd thing, and I couldn't explain it, not completely confident that I'd seen it. I was momentarily at a loss for words, which rarely happens to me.

A second later—no more than the beat of the heart—his face returned to the angry hard lines I'd seen before. If anything, he was possibly more unfriendly toward me, and I had no idea why.

"No interview," Liam barked as he climbed into the truck, closed the door, and started it up.

I looked at the brothers staring through the back window

with curious expressions. The darker haired brother winked at me as I watched them drive away.

I turned to Daisy with a bewildered look. "What the hell do you think that was about?" I asked.

I dealt with people who didn't wish to be interviewed all the time, but this was different. It felt *personal*, and that bothered me more than it should have.

"What did you do to him? I've never seen the McKenzie brothers run so fast. Damn, but that Seth is a handsome devil," Daisy said.

"Was he the dark-haired one?" I asked.

"Yep. That's him. He's hard to pin down. I've tried, and so have half the women in Flagstaff," Daisy said dreamily. "We had drinks one night. Made out like crazy, but he never called. Best night of my life."

Daisy didn't look offended, but I was indignant on her behalf. "I know that type. Not interested. What's Captain McKenzie's story?" I asked, curious about the rude, but undeniably sexy fire captain. Not that I'd give him the time of day, but I couldn't help wondering what he was like when he wasn't snarling like a pit-bull. Did he have a girlfriend? I didn't really care, just curious.

"Where have you been?" Daisy said, lugging the camera back to the news van. She was a petite woman so the camera may have weighed as much as she did. I had never touched the equipment because Daisy wouldn't allow it. She claimed it was delicate and should only be handled by a professional.

"The McKenzie brothers are the most sought-after bachelors in Flagstaff, and maybe even Sedona, for that matter. I mean, did you see them? They're excellent specimens of male sexuality at its finest. And there are three of them—in the same family!" Daisy placed the equipment in the back of the van, closed the doors, then leaned against them dramatically.

I admitted they were attractive, but I was only drawn to

Liam for some reason…a fact that bugged me, since he'd brushed me off so rudely.

"I'm not done with Liam McKenzie. If he doesn't answer my questions, I'll go through his brothers. If they won't help me, I'll talk to the fire chief. I helped him with a fundraiser for his granddaughter's school last month," I said, climbing into the van.

"Careful, he didn't seem to like you very much. I'd hate to see how he reacts if he's backed into a corner," Daisy said, starting the van.

I looked out the window as two stretchers with black body bags were carried from the forest and loaded into the coroner's van. They hadn't released the names, because the next of kin had not been notified, but the sheriff did confirm that both victims were twenty-six-years-old, one male, one female. Way too young to die, I'd thought sadly.

The deaths were classified as suspicious, pending further investigation. I wanted to tell their story. No matter what it was, they deserved that much.

As we drove out on the narrow dirt road, the only entrance to the small trailhead parking lot, we passed another van on the way to the scene. Daisy had to pull onto the narrow shoulder of the road to let them pass.

"Well, what do you know? Did we just get the drop on Brenda Jeffrey?" Daisy said slyly.

As if in slow motion, the other vehicle passed us. It was another KUTV news van. Inside were Brenda and her cameraman, Bernie. If looks could kill, I'd have been six feet under.

Brenda glared daggers at us when the vans passed. I decided to wave and pretend I didn't notice how pissed off she was that we'd beaten them to the scene. Daisy and I shared a high-five when the other van was out of sight.

I pulled out my laptop to start my story and send off the

preliminary report to my boss, Ken Turner, before Brenda could sink her claws in and claim it for herself. That woman was the bane of my existence, ever since I took the job at KUTV as a street reporter six months earlier.

More than a few times, Brenda seemed to arrive on the scene and steal the story right out from under me. I worked long hard hours, often sleeping with the police scanner next to my bed, just to catch the next story that could launch my career.

The problem was, nothing much ever happened in Flagstaff, but if I managed to shine enough with my humdrum news reports, I might be noticed and hopefully picked up by a national news channel in a large city. That was the game plan, anyway. I had become an expert at making the mundane happenings around town seem exceptional, or at least interesting when I reported on them.

On the drive back, I managed to get my copy off to the editing director, and then placed a call to my connection at the coroner's office.

"Hey, Eric, Jessica Parker here." I had him on speaker phone in the news van. Daisy rolled her eyes and slid her finger across her throat.

"Hey, Jessica. I was just thinking about you," Eric said.

Daisy and I rolled our eyes. Eric had been asking me out the entire six months I'd been in Flagstaff. He didn't take no for an answer, but his determination hadn't changed my mind, either.

"Oh, that's nice. Hey, Eric, I'm calling about the two campers they'll be bringing your way today. You've probably been given a heads-up, right?" I asked.

"Um, you know I can't share that information with you, Jessica."

"I'm not asking for much. I just want to hear the cause of

death before anyone else. Can you do that favor for me?" I begged.

"Well…as long as you don't ask me for any more detail before they're released. You can't quote me. It won't be official," Eric warned.

"Deal. I just need to know first, and I won't use your name," I assured him.

"Okay, how about lunch today?" Eric offered.

Daisy threw me a warning look and shook her head. I hesitated, chewing on my lower lip. I had no desire to have lunch with Eric because I knew he liked me and…well, I didn't like him. He was attractive enough, but there was zero chemistry on my side. Besides, I was too busy to date, anyway.

"Jessica, you still there? Jess?"

"Yes, yes. I'm still here. Sorry, I got distracted," Daisy snorted out a laugh. I gave her a dirty look. "Sure, I'll meet you for lunch. Where?"

Daisy slapped her own forehead. I motioned for her to watch the road.

"How about the Toasted Squirrel Cafe? At noon?"

I slumped in my seat. "Sure. See you then." The things I endured for my career.

"See you then," Eric said, a little too enthusiastically.

I ended the call. Daisy just shook her head. "Sucker."

"It's just lunch. It won't kill me. It's only an hour, right?" I said, possibly trying to convince myself more than Daisy.

"It's your hole to step into, not mine, but I'd step into it for you," Daisy added.

We had just arrived back to the KUTV news building. I stopped walking and stared at Daisy. "Wait. Do you have a thing for Eric?" I asked.

Daisy realized I had stopped walking, so she stopped. "Of course not. But he is kind of hot, even if he's not your type.

I'd go for it, but he's got a thing for you, so…" Daisy shrugged her shoulders like she didn't really care one way or another, but I felt terrible that I hadn't noticed or figured this out on my own.

"Maybe he would, if he knew you were interested," I said casually.

"Don't go turning Cupid on me. He's not interested, and I don't care," Daisy stated.

"Okay." I walked past Daisy after we entered the building and headed toward my cubicle. Only the anchors had actual offices. One day, I planned to have a real office.

"Wait, are you saying you'll drop it? Leave it alone?" Daisy jogged to catch up with me.

"Sure. If that's what you want," I said matter-of-factly.

Daisy looked unsure. I gave her a brilliant smile before slipping into my chair and opening my laptop. Daisy shrugged and went to the tech room, most likely to begin reviewing the footage for a couple of stories we were working on. I scribbled Daisy's and Eric's names on a post-it note and slipped it in my pocket.

I opened Google and typed *Liam McKenzie* into the browser. "Let's see what we can find on you, Captain Stick-up-your-butt." I smiled to myself, thinking how much I suspected he would hate that nickname.

One thing was for sure, Liam McKenzie had gotten under my skin somehow. I'd found it difficult to think of anything else.

4

*L*iam

We arrived at the fire station to relieve the crew who had covered for us. I managed to avoid one newspaper journalist and two other news channel reporters, all vying for the best scoop on the deceased campers.

I made it crystal clear that none of the McKenzies would be giving statements. The paramedics, Dave and Tyler, wanted details, so Seth filled them in with our modified version of events. It was the buzz around the station for a couple hours before it quickly became old news. Nothing like running emergency calls on a regular basis to desensitize someone to traumatic events.

I was glad the fuss had died down, but I couldn't help but feel concerned about the way the campers died. Was there a new monster among us? Was it still here? I needed to know how the hikers died. I had a bad feeling, like a dark cloud was hovering over my town.

My town. When had it become my town? We'd lived in Flagstaff, Arizona for almost eight years. Somewhere during that time, it became home. Even though the good people of

Flagstaff knew nothing of how different we were, they'd accepted us as their own.

I was in the office filling out reports for several minor calls we'd run that morning when Seth stuck his head in the door. "Guess who's calling again?"

I leaned back in the chair and looked up at the ceiling. "How many is that? It has to be a record."

Seth smirked, "Nine, but who's counting?"

I rubbed my hands across my face as if that might erase the tenacious blonde reporter from my mind and my growing list of possible problems.

"What do you want me to say?" Seth asked, looking amused.

I had begun to think Jessica Parker was not the sort of woman to be easily ignored. If she hadn't been such a thorn in my side, and so much wasn't at stake, I could have appreciated her tenacious spirit.

"I don't think she's going to go away, even if we ignore her," I said.

"Then maybe you meet her in the middle. You control the interview. It might get her off our backs, and it'll eventually blow over," Seth offered.

"You may be right, but I'm worried she'll keep digging."

"Or she might get her interview and happily move on to annoy someone new," Seth offered, and we both smiled.

"Okay, I'll take her call and set up an interview, but only me. I don't want her finding some small discrepancy in our individual accounts," I said, reaching for the phone on the desk.

"Or you just want to keep her all for yourself," Seth teased, leaving the office before I could respond.

I squeezed my eyes shut. When I opened them, I pushed the flashing light on the phone and answered, "Captain McKenzie."

There was a long pause, and I wondered if she'd hung up after waiting so long.

"Oh, Captain McKenzie. I didn't expect you to answer," Jessica said.

Her voice evoked the same physical reaction it had when she'd spoken earlier that morning. A strange feeling passed through me that I had no words for, and it instantly made me cross. I needed to bring my A-game with this woman.

"You called me, right?" There was a pause. "What can I do for you, Ms. Parker?" I asked, trying to make my tone neutral and detached.

"Yes, but since you refused to take any of my previous calls, it caught me off guard. Thank you, by the way."

"For what?" I asked.

"For taking my call. You'd really make my day if you'd let me interview you about the hikers," Jessica said.

"Fine."

Another pause. "Really?"

"No camera." I didn't want my face broadcast across the news channels. We'd done well to disappear from our past life. One interview could ruin everything my brothers and I had sacrificed in order to protect ourselves.

"Okay. I'll agree to those terms. When can we meet?" she asked.

"Meet me at the Burning Moon at eight tomorrow evening," I said.

Another pause. "All right. I'll meet you there. Thank you, Captain," she said.

I hung up the phone and began visualizing Jessica Parker sitting on a bar stool. I instantly regretted asking her to meet me there. This would be so much easier if I wasn't attracted to her—drawn to her, even.

Cole came into the office. "I heard you're meeting that reporter."

As usual, Cole was excited, which only made me second guess my decision some more. "Yes. We're meeting at the Burning Moon tomorrow."

"Sounds like a date," Cole said, grinning like he knew a secret.

"It's not like that. You, Seth, and I were going anyway. But don't get any ideas. I only agreed to an interview with me and no cameras. You and Seth are still under strict orders to avoid her," I added.

"I see what you're doing there," Cole said, wiggling his eyebrows at me.

The tones sounded throughout the station, signaling an emergency call coming in. We listened as a dispatcher's voice came over the intercom system. "Engine seven, medic seven, respond to west Phoenix Avenue and South Miles Pike. Unconscious person. Respond code 3, on F2."

Cole and I were already heading for the engine bay where the fire engine and medic trucks waited. Seth was already behind the wheel of the fire engine, and the large metal doors were rising as Cole and I stepped into our boots and pulled on our fire turnouts before climbing into the cab.

I pulled on the headset and adjusted the microphone. The head-sets protected our hearing and allowed us to communicate with dispatch, as well as one another, above the loud noise of the sirens and the engine itself.

The two medics were already pulling out of the bay, and we followed as Seth maneuver the engine out of the station.

It took us seven minutes from the time we received the call before we arrived on scene. Seth parked the engine so that it blocked traffic on the street, which lent some protection for the patient and my crew while the medics did an assessment.

Tyler looked up at me. "We have a code arrest."

One medic vigorously started chest compressions while

the other placed the defibrillation pads on the patient's torso. Cole moved in to take over compressions to free Dave to help evaluate the patient's heart rhythm.

"Patient is in V-fib. We have a shockable rhythm," Tyler announced. "Charging. Clear." Everyone stopped what they were doing, careful not to touch the patient. The man's body jerked and lifted off the ground briefly from the shock.

Dave put his stethoscope to the patient's chest. "We got a pulse."

"Okay, let's move now," Tyler said.

Seth had already brought the gurney, in case it was needed.

The patient was quickly prepared for transport and loaded into the medic truck. Cole drove them so that the paramedics could work on the patient in the back. Seth and I stayed a few minutes more to collect more information and answer some brief questions from his wife and daughter. There were many bystanders milling about, and even more, watching from nearby restaurants., in particular, caught my attention as I prepared to climb up into the engine and return to the station.

Jessica Parker sat at the cafe patio across the street with a man. I felt hot all over and knew my wolf was stirring. Jessica and I made eye contact briefly before I climbed into the engine's cab.

Did she have a boyfriend? It made sense. I hadn't noticed a ring, so I figured they weren't married. I glared at the other man as if I had some claim to Jessica. It was doubtful the man could even tell I was throwing lethal daggers his way, but Jessica noticed. Her delicate eyebrows had scrunched together as she most likely tried to understand my behavior.

That made two of us. I didn't understand my reaction to seeing her with another man any more than she did. I had no claim on her and absolutely no intentions to act on my attraction. That ship could never sail. I wasn't what she needed.

It wasn't like I could afford a relationship, anyway. I was forced to give up the woman I'd loved long ago because leaving was the only way I knew to protect her from the curse my brothers and I shared. We still didn't understand it. After eight years, we were no closer to understanding why we shifted. *Eight years since we'd seen another shifter.*

I considered canceling my meeting with Jessica, but I knew she would keep coming if I did. That much I had gathered from our brief interactions.

I'd keep the meeting if only to be done with the entire business so I could stop thinking about every detail of her face.

THE REST of the twenty-four-hour shift was quiet, and we managed to sleep all night without a single call. Sometimes, we got lucky like that. That morning, my brothers and I stood around talking to the members of the crew as they arrived to relieve us.

"Breakfast at the Squirrel, anyone?" Cole asked.

"Not this morning, but I'll see you both tonight," Seth said.

"See you at the Moon, Seth," Cole said.

The Moon was the nickname for The Burning Moon Bar that we frequented. It was a favorite with locals and sat on a corner along the main drag in the historic part of town. Walking into The Moon felt like stepping back in time, and it was my favorite spot to have a few beers and play some pool.

"See you, Seth," I said.

"I'll be late, but I'll be there," added Seth, as he climbed onto his motorcycle and pulled a slick black helmet over his head. It was the same bike that had once belonged to the shifter I had killed. The same night we'd learned what we were. It changed our lives in ways we could never have imagined. It certainly changed our direction.

The biker and his pack had known what we were before we did. In a cruel twist of fate, it was also the night we lost our father to a massive heart attack. I still carried not only the guilt of taking a life but the painful suspicion that the heart attack may have been brought on when our pa witnessed me turning into a wolf before his eyes.

Cole and I watched Seth pulled out of the fire station parking lot. I assumed he was heading home to his apartment above the automotive repair shop. The owner allowed him to tinker with his vintage truck or his motorcycle whenever he wanted.

"What do you say, Liam?" Cole persisted.

"Sure, let's see what Old Henry is serving up today," I said.

Cole lived in a small house he owned, located directly north of the college campus. Being the youngest, he enjoyed the energy of the neighborhood, since it was mostly filled with students. He nodded and climbed into his hard-topped Jeep, and I got into my old Ford truck that I'd had since high school. I could afford a new vehicle, but I preferred the simplicity and style of the older models.

THE TOASTED SQUIRREL was always busy, but only for breakfast and lunch. It had an eclectic style that felt like you just walked into a yard sale from the seventies. You might find old metal bird cages with plants in them or macramé owls or other creatures. Squirrels were the theme. There several live ones, who lived off the patio food, almost year-round.

Henry, the owner and head cook at the Toasted Squirrel, was a middle-aged Navajo Native American, with long jet-black hair he kept pulled back with a leather tie and a feather hanging down. I once asked him if it meant anything special, and he laughed and said he wore it for the tourists, but I suspected there was more to it than that. Henry was fiercely proud of his ancestry.

Henry spotted us standing in line, while we waited for our turn to be seated. He stopped what he was doing, wiped his hands on his apron, and came over to greet us.

"I got your table ready, boys. Follow me," he said, ushering us past the line of people waiting. He took us to the furthest corner of the dining room. No matter how busy he was, Henry always made time to treat Seth, Cole, and me like special guests. Henry regarded all first responders and military with respect. We appreciated the special attention Henry, and his staff afforded us.

"Just getting off shift?" Henry asked as he handed us menus.

"Yep. It was an easy one. How are you, Henry?" Cole asked.

"Working myself into an early grave. Other than that, I can't complain," he joked.

"And the grandkids? What will they do if PoP-PoP keels over? You should take it easy. Let someone else do the heavy lifting for a change," I urged. It was true that he took on too much himself. It was a hard life running a successful restaurant.

"They're good, and they'll be set for college," he said, laughing as he headed back to the kitchen. "Stephany will be over to take your order in a few."

"Thanks, Henry," I said.

"Can we talk about what happened?" Cole asked, lowering his voice and looking around.

"Can I eat first?"

Cole shrugged and began to study his menu. I don't know why he bothered. He always ordered the buckwheat pancakes with bacon and hash browns.

I DROVE SOUTH ON I-17, in the direction of Sedona until I exited on the 89A. My home was fifteen easy miles from town, between Sedona and Flagstaff. My land was secluded and nestled among the forest. I'd been living in a fifth-wheel travel trailer while I worked on the cabin I'd been building, almost entirely by myself. Seth and Cole would lend a hand when I needed help.

It was an excellent way to spend my spare time. The location was also ideal for trail running, which I did often. Some days I'd stop by the jiu-jitsu gym near the fire station. Staying busy kept the loneliness at bay.

Staying busy kept my mind away from more troubling questions, such as our mysterious past that I'd assumed, by this point, would never be solved. But that didn't stop the nagging questions from haunting my thoughts. I'd suspected it was something we all still struggled with from time to time, but we no longer talked about it.

As usual, I worked hard until it was time to meet my brothers and Jessica at the bar. I couldn't seem to get the woman out of my head. Her face was haunting me. Thinking hard, I tried to recall a time when a woman had affected me this way. I couldn't think of any, except for Harmony, my high school sweetheart. That had been the closest, but still, this seemed different. My interest in Harmony grew over time.

When I discovered what I was, I left Harmony, hoping to

protect her. She never knew why—only that I broke her heart.

I'd learned through my lawyer, that she had graduated college at Berkeley, started some business that organized and guided the finances of restaurants, married her business partner, and had her first child last year.

I was happy for her. This was why I left—so she could have a normal life. I was able to let go of Harmony once I learned she was settled and apparently happy.

I thought about seeing Jessica with that other man, and I was suddenly seething again. At that moment, there was nothing I wanted more than to rip the other guy apart. *What the hell was wrong with me?* I had recently shifted, so I should have been more relaxed. Sometimes we were edgy when we hadn't shifted for a few weeks. It was like a necessary form of therapy.

Mine. A strange thought kept speaking into my head. I clamped down hard on my inner wolf when it wanted to say, *Jessica is mine.* I'd never been the jealous type, not even with Harmony. And this woman would never be mine. A relationship wasn't in the cards for me, even if I acknowledged the desire to be with her was incredibly strong.

That morning, I went for a long trail run. My plan was to shove Jessica out of my head with physical exhaustion. It worked for a while but didn't last nearly long enough.

Finally, I gave up and prepared to meet my brothers, and the woman haunting my thoughts.

Jessica was a news reporter, damn it. I'd need to be careful around her.

5

The sun had set by the time I arrived at the Burning Moon. The bar had been a mainstay of Flagstaff history, even though the name changed several times over the past hundred years. We'd only known it as the Burning Moon. The bar's furnishings seemed to have been frozen in time. Everything was highly polished dark-stained wood, from the bar, floor, ceiling, and even paneling on the walls. The only modern elements were one pool table and several neon signs that hung in the front windows and above the bar.

Cole sat on a stool near the only pool table. For the moment, the table was being used by some other guys. No doubt Cole had already put coins down to claim the next game. He was looking at something on his phone when I walked up to the bar and stood next to him.

"Anything interesting?" I asked.

Cole looked up and greeted me with a wide, boyish smile. "Hey, Liam. No, I was just looking for information about those campers."

"Find anything?" I asked

"Nope. Nothing that we didn't already know. What'd you do today?" Cole put his phone in his pocket and took a sip of his beer.

"I did some trail running and worked on installing a window in the cabin," I said.

"How's the cabin coming along? Have you gotten much done since I helped run the wiring?" he asked.

"Most of the windows are in," I said, looking down the bar. Another bartender was just coming on shift. Her name was Zoey Bannon. She'd only been working at the bar for the last month or so.

Cole had a massive crush on Zoey, but he said she gave off the *not-available* vibe whenever he tried to flirt, so he reluctantly settled for admiring from afar.

Seth also had tried to hit on Zoey when she first showed up, but she shot him down without batting an eye. Once Cole saw his older brother crash and burn, he figured there was no hope for him.

Women seemed to love Seth, even though none of them could make him stick around. I didn't know if he stayed single because of choice, like me, or hadn't met anyone he could share our secret with. Were there women who could love someone like us? I couldn't imagine it.

Zoey noticed me waiting and came to take my order as she tied a small black apron around her hips.

"Hello, boys. What'll you have, Liam?" She was good with names and quick with a friendly smile. Zoey's hair was long waves of molten lava. Every shade of red with dark undertones of auburn woven together to make one pretty redhead.

"I'll have that new IPA you have on tap," I said.

It was almost painful to watch how nervous Cole would get when Zoey was tending bar. I wished he'd just ask her out, but I knew Cole was afraid she'd reject him like she had every other guy who'd tried. She was lovely, and I understood Cole's attraction, but his skin was not as thick as Seth's or mine, which made him more cautious.

"Coming right up. You good, Cole?" Zoey asked.

Cole's voice almost cracked when he replied. "Yeah, I mean yes. I'm good for now. Thanks for asking," Cole stammered. Zoey smiled at him and turned to get my beer.

Cole rolled his eyes and slapped his forehead with the palm of his hand.

"Take it easy, Cole. You just need to relax around her. Let her get to know what a great guy you are," I said quietly. He looked at me with a pained look.

"Table's yours," said one of the men who'd been playing pool.

I nodded, and Cole slid off his stool and began to rack the balls for our game. Zoey brought my beer, then went back behind the bar to serve other patrons.

We were almost through the first game when Jessica and her friend entered the bar. A whistle came from a group of men in a corner booth that both women ignored as they made their way toward Cole and me.

I instantly felt hostile toward the men. So much so, I had to focus on controlling my breathing and commanded my wolf to relax. What the devil was wrong with me? Why was I feeling this way?

Jessica walked up to me smiling confidently, with the other woman coming to stand next to her. Tonight, both women wore jeans. Jessica had on high wedged shoes, while the other woman wore checked Converse. They were both attractive, but extreme opposites by comparison.

Jessica walked right up and extended her hand while giving me a warm but cautious smile. "Thank you for meeting with me, Captain McKenzie."

I hesitated a moment, then reached for her hand. When we touched, a shock, like before, ran up my arm. I couldn't hide my surprised reaction. She snatched her hand away as we awkwardly stared at one another.

"What happened?" Cole asked.

Jessica was rubbing her hand on her jeans. I just stared at her.

Seth's loud voice interrupted the strange moment. "I'm here. What did I miss?" Seth asked, sauntering up to Jessica and her friend.

He noticed the tension and looked between Jessica and me. Nobody answered him. "Obviously, I've missed something." He laughed and then headed to the bar. "Zoey, my love, could I have a whiskey and Coke, please?" Zoey nodded and pulled down the single barrel whiskey she knew Seth preferred.

Jessica and I had recovered somewhat, or at least we pretended to, by the time Seth joined us again.

"These are my brothers, Seth and Cole." Cole and Seth stepped forward to shake hands with Jessica. Seth went as far as to kiss the back of Jessica's hand. He threw me a challenging smirk as he did. I squeezed my fists at my sides and tried to pretend his taunt didn't bother me. At least Jessica seems to be immune to Seth's charms.

"This is my friend and coworker, Daisy Thorp.

I shook Daisy's hand.

"Hey, Daisy," Seth said, drawing out her name and putting his arm around her shoulders as if they were old friends.

"Seth," Daisy replied. She looked pleased with the attention Seth was giving her.

I gave him a warning look, but he merely smiled and ignored me, as if I were a nagging parent.

"Seth, you can finish my game. I'll be at the bar with Ms. Parker," I said, motioning for Jessica to precede me to the bar.

"Jessica or Jess. My friends call me Jess," she volunteered

as she brushed past me on the way to the bar. She climbed onto a stool and made herself comfortable.

"You can call me Liam," I said, appreciating the view of her backside as she walked ahead of me. Jessica had a small waist with full round hips and butt that were stuffed into snug jeans that made my thoughts go in directions best not pondered, under the circumstances.

Her mood seemed to brighten, and I wondered again if I were making a critical mistake by agreeing to the interview. Just being that close to her had me humming with wolf energy that I struggled to manage. I prided myself on the level of control I'd developed over my wolf nature. How could one woman threaten that with no more than a smile?

Jessica had a notepad and pen with her. She opened the pad and held her pen at the ready. I sat on the stool next to hers. There wasn't much room, so when our knees touched, I almost expected a similar reaction to when I'd felt her hand, but there was none—just a hyper-awareness of her closeness. She glanced down at our knees touching and then up at me. She smiled nervously. That was a change. Jessica had exuded nothing but confidence since we'd crossed paths. Could it be that I made her nervous?

"So, I'll get right to it. What were you and your brothers doing in that part of the forest on the morning you discovered the campers?" She had her pen poised as if taking notes for a class.

"We were returning to my truck after camping," I said, without elaborating.

Jessica nodded and scribbled something on her pad. "If you had to guess, how far away were the bodies from your camp?" she asked, still writing.

"About a mile north." I leaned back and crossed my arms over my chest. I hoped the interrogation didn't last long. I had an overwhelming desire to hold her in my arms and kiss the sense out of her.

I'd always found smart women attractive, and like most men, I had a regular healthy sex drive, but this was not normal. I was not that possessive sex-crazed guy who acted on every urge.

"And you heard nothing that night, while you were camping a less than a mile away?" Jessica stopped scribbling to look at me.

"Like what?" I countered. I didn't like how her tone switched from friendly to all business in a heartbeat.

Jessica held my gaze. "Like screams or shouting? Two people died violently. I know that I'd be screaming."

I stared at her for a moment. "You can't know how you'd react for certain."

She shifted nervously on her stool. "You're right. I don't know for sure, but--"

"No. We heard nothing like that," I lied. I couldn't know if we'd heard anything or not after we shifted. Sometimes flashes of memories were clear, but other times they were a jumble of images that didn't always go together.

"You and your brothers camp often?" she asked.

"Yes." I took a sip of my beer, still watching her.

"In that particular area?" she pressed.

"Yes." I could tell my short answers were starting to annoy her.

"Why? Why that area? Aren't there better areas to camp in these mountains?"

"Why not? We like to avoid the crowds and prefer to be alone," I replied. "Campgrounds are too tame for our tastes," I challenged.

"Too tame, huh? You and your brothers like to walk on the wild side. I get it. It's a guy thing, right? Man against nature—that sort of thing?" she asked innocently.

I nodded once. If she'd only known, she'd probably have run out of there screaming.

Jessica paused to call Zoey over. "I'll take a margarita, please—on the rocks and easy on the salt."

Zoey nodded to Jessica, then smirked at me before turning away. I wondered how much of the conversation she'd overheard.

When Jessica turned her attention back to me, she smiled her friendly smile again, as if she hadn't just asked me a bunch of accusatory questions that hinted at a cover-up.

"So, you're antisocial, preferring to be alone in the wilderness so you can what—howl at the moon in peace?" I choked on my beer.

I apologized and glanced over at my brothers, who were standing around the pool table with Daisy. Seth gave me a strange look, probably wondering what was going on. I was wondering the same thing.

"I think this interview is over. I hope you got what you came for, Ms. Parker," I said, standing.

Jessica looked surprised, holding the margarita Zoey had just placed in front of her. "But I haven't asked all of my questions," Jessica said, following me to the pool table.

I stopped and turned around. She must have been right on my heels because she almost ran into me. We were so close, our bodies were only inches away from each other.

Staring into her blue eyes made me want to dive into their depths and happily drown there. "I'm done. If you'd like to stay and shoot some pool, feel free, but I don't care to be interviewed anymore. You'll have to get your story some-place else." She blinked up at me several times before I walked away. I picked up a pool stick and began rubbing the tip with the blue cube of chalk.

"But—" she started to protest.

"I'll buy your next drink," I said, bending over to take the first shot of a new game.

Jessica pressed her lips into a thin line of frustration. Daisy wiggled her eyebrows at her suggestively. Seth and Cole watched her with big grins on their faces.

If I didn't know any better, I'd guess this was a mutiny on both sides. I hadn't missed how the curly-haired brunette had been flirting with Seth, maybe Cole too.

I watched as Jessica seemed to consider her options until she blew out a heavy sigh. She tipped her drink back and finished half the margarita in seconds. I smiled to myself. I needed to be careful around Jessica, but my wolf was happy she was sticking around for a while.

As Jessica sauntered over and took a pool stick out of Seth's hands, I motioned to Zoey for another round. If I was playing with fire, I might as well have some fun. *What harm could come from a game of pool?*

I took the first shot, breaking up the cluster of balls and sending three into various pockets. "I'll take stripes," I said, before sinking two more balls. When I missed my next shot, I stepped away from the table so that Jessica could assess her next move. "Ever played before?"

"Not much," Jess said, lining up her shot. She laid over the table to reach the ball she wanted and sunk the red solid in the corner pocket.

Seth made a too-hot motion by fanning himself, causing Cole and Daisy to crack up. Jessica ignored them all and lined up and made two more shots.

I was impressed. She didn't look like a woman who spent time playing pool, but she certainly knew what she was doing. Playing pool with her could be addicting. She was making me all kinds of crazy each time she bent over the table. I had the distinct impression that she knew how she was affecting me and maybe, enjoyed it.

When she finally missed, it was my turn. I lined up my shot, pulled the stick back, and froze. Seth and Cole were instantly on alert as well. I narrowed my eyes as I watched a man walk into the bar—*only it wasn't a man.*

The stranger's hair was jet black and he wore it slicked back. His face was sharply chiseled and hinted at a European heritage, Italian maybe. The man wore a button shirt that was fashionably untucked, designer jeans, and fancy steel-tipped boots. He had a movie-star quality that stuck out like a sore thumb in a laid-back mountain town like this.

I knew immediately that he wasn't human, and so did Seth and Cole. As I straightened up, my brothers instinctively moved closer, standing on either side of me. The man with the light blue eyes zeroed in on us as well. He stood there, taking our measure. There was pure, unmasked hatred in his eyes.

It was clear that whatever he was, he knew what we were, which put us at a severe disadvantage. Breaking through the tension, Zoey, carrying a tray of drinks, seemed to walk out of her way to step in front of the man, which broke his intense focus on us.

"Sit wherever you like. I'll be right with you."

Then Zoey walked directly to the pool table, she wriggled herself closer to me so that Seth had to move out of her way to make room for the big tray of drinks she was carrying. She began handing the bottles around, but as she handed the last one to me, she held onto it, until she caught my attention.

Zoey's gaze bore into me with such intensity. "Easy, Liam. You don't need that particular breed of trouble," she said in a low voice, apparently meant only for me.

6

*J*essica

I couldn't help but notice the hostile reaction from the McKenzie brothers when the dark-haired man walked into the bar. The stranger seemed to have a similar response to the family trio as well. *Did they know each other?*

And what was up with Zoey? I could be wrong, but the pretty bartender may have been flirting with Liam. I'd always liked Zoey, but when I watched her snuggle in tight to whisper something that only Liam could hear, I couldn't help but feel a twinge of jealousy.

It didn't help that he stared after her so intently that I felt green with envy. *I was not that girl.* I did not get jealous over guys' attention…especially not Liam McKenzie.

I may be attracted to his completely addictive male sexuality, but that didn't mean I was stupid enough to want more from him than an interview. I had tried in vain to find any concrete information on the man. He'd somehow burrowed under my skin and was now a constant itch I could only dream of scratching.

I watched curiously as Zoey took her empty tray back behind the bar before walking over to the man. The newcomer had chosen a booth next to the door and was now openly staring at our group. Zoey said something to him, and him to her. She left and returned with a glass of red wine, then went about her business.

"Are we going to play or what?" I asked, apparently not seeing what the fuss was about and feeling a touch annoyed at the thought of Zoey flirting with Liam—even though I had no right nor good reason.

Liam finally pulled his gaze away from Zoey, who he'd been staring at with an odd expression ever since she spoke to him. Liam lined up his next shot and missed.

***

AFTER SEVERAL MORE GAMES AND drinks, the mood had loosened somewhat. The brothers continued to steal glances at the man, and the man continued to openly stare at them while he sipped his wine and ordered another. I noticed that he didn't seem to be meeting anyone, and I thought it odd he was so focused on our group.

Eventually, I decided that the man was trying to entice the brothers into a fight, which I found totally unacceptable. I had maybe one margarita too many and found myself getting up from my stool to march, or perhaps sway, toward his table.

Suddenly, Liam was in front of me, staring down at me with such intensity I thought he must be looking right into my soul. But then I realized he was blocking my way on purpose. That was when I became annoyed.

"What are you doing, Liam?" I realized saying his name out loud felt very familiar and somewhat intimate.

Liam put a firm but gentle hand on my arm. "What are you doing, Ms. Parker?"

I looked up at him defiantly. Yes, I was buzzed I'd regret that tomorrow for a multitude of reasons. Even though he was treating me like a child, I found it difficult to keep myself from kissing him. He was way into my personal space, and it made all my senses come alive. I hadn't missed the way he chose to use my formal name, though.

The troublemaking man was watching us with an amused smirk. This made me even angrier. It had been my intention to give him a piece of my mind until Liam had interfered.

"I'm going to let this guy know how ridiculous he is for trying to incite a fight with you and your brothers." I was impressed that I managed to articulate my intentions without slurring my words—too much.

"Let's go back over to the table and finish our game," Liam suggested, attempting to turn me around.

"What—"

"Let the lady have her say," came the lightly accented voice of the man.

Liam whipped around so fast I had to step back. Now I couldn't see anything past his broad back and shoulders, so I bent down by his waist to look at the man. He was now standing next to the booth. *Wow, that escalated quickly.*

"You should leave," Liam said, his voice guttural and rough.

The next thing I knew, Cole and Seth were there, standing on either side of Liam, and I still hadn't gotten a word in. Daisy came up behind me and placed a hand on my shoulder. "Let's move away, Jess. This might get ugly, and you're in the line of fire."

I decided to heed my friend's advice. We walked back to our table.

"Am I not welcome here?" asked the man.

I thought his eyes seemed to be lighter than before. They were already unusually bright.

"No," Seth replied. Gone was the darker brother's playful nature.

"Pity. I was hoping to make the acquaintance of the lovely ladies over there," he said, nodding in the direction of Daisy and me.

Liam made a sound that could have been mistaken for a growl as he lunged for the man. Cole and Seth grabbed their older brother before he could do something we might all regret.

The stranger laughed mockingly. I began to wonder if the guy had a death wish. Hmm, death by McKenzie had a nice ring to it. I almost laughed at my own silly thought.

"Good idea, keeping him on a leash," the man said.

He was gorgeous. There was no doubt about that, but something about his gaze was predatory and made me feel nervous. Maybe it was a good thing Liam hadn't let me reach the man. I shivered.

"I'll be seeing you around, Ms. Parker," the man said, then winked and blew a kiss my way. Cole and Seth could hardly contain Liam after that. The man left, but it took several moments for Liam to calm down. I watched and waited while his brothers whispered urgently to him. After a few moments, they released him and stepped cautiously away.

Seth turned a charming grin our way as if that whole tense scene hadn't happened. Cole put away the cue sticks and went to settle the tab with Zoey at the bar.

I stared at Liam's back until he finally turned around and moved slowly toward us. When he was closer, he said, "I'd like to see you safely home."

I was instantly jolted into sobriety with his unexpected request.

"Ummm…" I wasn't sure if it was such a good idea for me

to be alone with Liam.

"I drove her," Daisy said.

Seth slipped his arm around Daisy's shoulders. "I was just about to ask if I could see you safely home," Seth said, offering Daisy a swoon-worthy smile.

Daisy melted like butter before glancing anxiously at me. "Is that okay? Do you want me to take you home instead?" Daisy asked, but her eyes told another story. I knew she wanted to be alone with Seth and I didn't want to be the one who ruined Daisy's chance with the playboy firefighter, even if I thought it was a mistake.

"Sure," I said. Daisy's smile made her look younger than she was.

"It was sort of creepy how that guy knew your name," Daisy added.

"I'm on the news every night. It's not a stretch to assume he recognized me," I said.

I thought it was creepy too, but didn't want to make a big deal out of it. But now I was going to be alone with a man who made my heart skip beats and the butterflies flutter in my stomach. The same man I'd already decided was not dating material. Besides, he didn't even like me and had made that crystal clear. *So, why did he want to see me home?*

I figured the male posturing had little to do with me, and more to do with the combination of male egos, testosterone, and beer. I knew better than to flatter myself over Liam's seemingly protective behavior.

I hugged Daisy goodbye and whispered in her ear to behave herself. Daisy just winked and headed out of the bar with Seth. Liam picked up my purse and handed it to me. He looked somewhat embarrassed and uncomfortable. Could he be regretting his macho behavior?

"I need to ask Cole something. Do you mind waiting for a moment?" Liam asked.

I shook my head and watched him walk over to the bar where Cole was settling the tab with Zoey. Liam said something to his brother and then leaned across the bar to say something to Zoey. She listened then looked over at me. I was starting to feel like there was a joke that I didn't get.

Liam walked up to me and put his hand on the small of my back as he guided me past the booth where the man had sat, out of the bar, and onto the busy street. Since this was a college town, there were always groups of people moving from one place to another. Tonight was no exception.

We passed several clusters of loud partiers on the way to Liam's truck. It was parked a couple of blocks away from the restaurants and bars on a quiet, dark residential street. Liam seemed to be hyper-aware of our surroundings. Maybe he was really concerned about that guy jumping us.

He opened the passenger-side door for me, but his eyes never stopped roaming the street and shadowy yards. Once he was in the truck, he seemed to relax some, but not entirely.

I told him my address, and he seemed to know where it was, so I let my head relax against the seat and might have dozed off during the ride. It seemed like we were at my small home on Baker Street way too quickly.

I'd barely opened my eyes before Liam was opening my door and offering me his hand. Nothing weird happened when we touched this time, *for which I was thankful.*

Liam walked me to my front door. I had an automatic light sensor on the porch that turned on when it became dark. I unlocked my door and turned to thank him for the drinks and the ride home. When I looked up at him, my breath caught.

I may have been imagining it, but the look in his eyes seemed to be raw animalistic passion, and it made me want to melt into a puddle right there on my porch.

My mouth went dry, and my lips parted, but no words would come. Liam's gaze was focused on my lips. He slowly lowered his head and our lips met, it was like someone threw lighter fluid on my flames.

I let my bag slide down my arm until it gently thudded onto the ground and then slipped my arms around his thick chest, reveling in the firm feeling of his muscles. I could feel his arms surrounding me possessively, and nothing had ever felt better. His mouth burned a trail of kisses down my throat and then back up to claim my lips once more. I felt like I was meant to be here, in this man's arms for eternity.

What?

The strange thought was so foreign to me that it was like someone threw ice water on me. I gasped and pulled back, trying desperately to catch my breath and think clearly. I don't know if Liam could see my blush, but I could feel the heat rising in my cheeks.

Liam seemed to be trying to get a hold of himself, as well. He was breathing like he'd run a race. After an uncomfortable moment of silence, he said, "I'm sorry. I shouldn't have—"

"I was way out of line. I'm the one who should be apologizing. I asked to interview you, not attack you," I interrupted him. "Maybe we can just forget this ever happened."

Liam's face looked conflicted in the porch light. "Be sure to lock your doors, Ms. Parker. Good night." He turned so abruptly that I didn't know how to respond, but I knew how I felt—regret, longing, desperate. His walking away felt so wrong that I had to bite my tongue to keep from asking him to stay.

I'd never had this sort of reaction to a man. It felt different, and that made me nervous and excited at the same time. I turned and went into my home that suddenly felt lonely for the first time since moving to Flagstaff.

7

I woke to the sound of upbeat music playing on my phone. I slapped at the offending noise, and it fell off my nightstand and onto the floor. Groping around the edge of the bed, I found it and shut it off.

My head felt like someone used it for soccer practice, and I wanted to pull the covers over my eyes and hide from the approaching day. Beyond the window, I knew it was still dark. I always rose before the sun.

Mornings were usually my best time of day, but a severe hangover was a sure way to cramp my normal rhythm. I wasn't a big drinker, but I sort of knew I was having too much fun the night before. Or it may have been that Liam McKenzie made me nervous. It was usually me making guys nervous, not the other way around.

I dragged myself from the bed and managed to make it into the bathroom, I looked in the mirror and wondered what was different about Liam. He was handsome, but I'd been around attractive men. Hell, I worked in television. I'd even dated a few.

There was his animal-like magnetism that was almost a

tangible thing. That was different from other men. It seemed to radiate from him, and I didn't believe he was aware of the effect he had on the opposite sex.

And then there was that kiss. I hadn't expected that. Not with the way he'd acted toward me. Maybe it wasn't me, but the idea of an interview. Perhaps I was taking it personally, and it just wasn't.

It had felt personal. But then again, so had that kiss.

IT WAS ALMOST time for Daisy to pick me up for work. We'd been carpooling since my first week. It was this extra time together outside of work that had kindled our friendship.

I had just finished filling two travel mugs with homemade caramel macchiatos when I noticed the pencil drawing I'd done before going to bed last night.

It was a good likeness of the man in the bar. I slipped it into my briefcase in case it was ever needed. I grabbed the two coffees, then looked out the front window to see if Daisy had arrived. The sun had risen, but just barely. My heart skipped a beat. Liam's truck was still parked in front of my house.

I could see someone on the driver's side, so I poured an extra coffee and walked out to the truck to make sure he was okay. As I approached the truck, I tried to tell my heart to slow down. It wasn't listening as our kiss kept invading my thoughts.

When I reached the window on the driver's side, I could see Liam was sleeping. Hesitating, I studied his resting face. He looked gentler, almost innocent with his hard lines relaxed in sleep. I wanted to touch his face. It stirred something in me that I didn't understand.

Feeling guilty for watching him, I gently tapped on the

window with my travel mug. Liam jerked awake, and his eyes darted around quickly. He seemed to realize where he was, and then he saw me. He rubbed his hands over his face.

Liam looked embarrassed, and maybe angry again. Why did I keep having that effect on him? His face turned to hard lines, and his eyebrows knotted together. It was like a mask he dropped into place for the rest of the world, or maybe just for me.

Liam rolled the window down and grumbled, "Good morning."

I almost laughed as I handed him a cup of coffee. He looked surprised but took it from me.

"Thank you." He took a sip and his eyes closed for a few seconds as he seemed to savor the flavor. I must have guessed right. I served it to him black and strong. I didn't want to ruin his moment, so I took a sip from my travel mug and waited. When his eyes opened, he looked at me.

"Are you going to tell me why you're sleeping in your truck? You're wearing the same clothes from last night, so I'll assume you never left," I said, before taking another sip.

He looked down at the cup. "I was worried about that stranger last night."

That was not what I expected to hear. I thought maybe he decided he'd had too much to drink and slept it off in the truck. This…*this was sweet.* I was touched. Who does that sort of thing these days?

"You were concerned…" I tried to finish the thought.

"I had a bad feeling about him, and just wanted to be sure you were safe." Liam continued to sip his coffee and avoided making eye contact with me.

"Why didn't you say anything to me? I asked, still trying to understand this man. He was a puzzle, and I felt compelled to find the missing pieces.

"I didn't want to make too big a deal out of it. That

might have given you the wrong idea," he said, finally looking at me. His words said one thing, but his eyes held that same passion I'd seen the night before. I was getting mixed signals from Liam, and I wasn't entirely convinced he knew he was sending them. Or did he? Maybe I'd just imagined the whole thing, and the only passion was in my head.

"I see. Well, I can see how you wouldn't want me thinking that you liked me or anything like that," I said, unable to hide the irritation in my voice. I couldn't help it. I got his message, loud and clear.

Liam looked like he regretted his words, and then just seemed plain uncomfortable. He finished his coffee and handed the mug back to me. I took it, but feeling hurt, I found I couldn't look at him anymore. He hadn't even denied it.

He started his truck. "Thank you for the coffee, and…I'm sorry," he said, before pulling away from the curb and driving down the street. I just stood there feeling miserable. We weren't anything to each other, yet his driving away felt like breaking up. As silly as the thought was, it still left me feeling sad, hurt, and angry.

Daisy pulled up in her car, her eyes wide. She lowered her window and stared at me. "Was that Liam McKenzie leaving your house?"

"Not really. Give me a second, and I'll grab your coffee."

I returned from the house with my briefcase, her coffee drink, and a painting with a bow on it, under my arm.

"You did it! Oh, let me see," Daisy exclaimed, as I got into the car and handed her the coffee and the painting.

"He looks like my little Buttercup. Thank you, Jess. I love it," Daisy said, admiring the painting I'd made for her. She'd told me about losing her beloved Beagle last year, and how much she missed him. So, for a late birthday gift, I borrowed a picture of her dog and painted a portrait of Buttercup for Daisy.

"I hoped you'd like it," I said, putting on my seatbelt.

She turned to me with glossy eyes. "This is the nicest thing anyone has ever done for me," she said, and reached across the car and hugged me.

"It's therapy for me, so thank you for letting me paint him. I wish I'd known him."

"You really are talented, Jess. I don't know why you're a reporter. You're such a good artist. I mean it. It looks so professional," Daisy said, admiring the painting.

I laughed. "It's not that great, and it doesn't pay the bills, just ask my parents.

When I was young, I dreamed of painting for a living. There were few things I loved more than art. My parents began discouraging me from any serious aspiration and made certain that it was only to be a hobby. It had always been my outlet, a happy place to go when life got crazy. My house was filled with my paintings. Some girls collected dolls —I collected art, mostly mine.

Daisy carefully put the painting in the backseat then backed out of the drive.

"Okay, don't think that giving me a gift will get you off the hook. Liam stayed the night?" Daisy asked with renewed excitement.

I gave her a dry look. "It wasn't like that. I didn't even know he was here. Liam slept in his truck because he was worried about that guy last night."

Daisy began to drive. "That's it?"

I debated telling her about the kiss for all of three seconds. "And he kissed me when he walked me to the door." I stared straight ahead, but in my peripheral vision, I could see Daisy stealing glances at me. I wished she'd watch the road.

"Oh crap! You kissed Liam McKenzie." She was way too excited about that.

I decided to change the subject. "And what about you and Seth? What happened there?" I really did want to know.

"Nothing. He was a perfect gentleman. Damn it," she said, sounding deflated. "Seth kissed me on the cheek. I hope your kiss was less platonic."

With Seth's reputation and their prior make-out session, I'd assumed her night would be a bit more colorful than that. "Sorry," I offered.

"It's no big deal. I don't know what Seth's type is, but I already knew I wasn't it," she said, throwing me a genuine smile. It went a long way to tell me she really wasn't hurt by Seth's lack of interest.

So why did Liam's rejection feel like the end of something we didn't have, I wondered?

LIAM WASN'T the only one who had a bad feeling about the stranger in the bar. Stories for me usually began with a tip or nothing more than a question, and sometimes simply a gut feeling.

There had been two, so far, unexplained deaths in this small community where nothing too exciting ever happened. And in walks a stranger who sticks out like a sore thumb. I did consider the notion that he could be a wealthy student from another country, but he looked too old to be a student. Northern Arizona University or NAU, as we fondly referred to the state college, had plenty of foreign students coming and going.

But the man from last night neither struck me as a student, nor someone on vacation here to take on the great outdoors. He seemed too...something.

I was sitting at my desk considering all the possible ways the campers might have died. My contact at the morgue had not called with the official cause of death, so all my ideas were loose notions for the moment.

Daisy stuck her head around my cubicle. "Want to grab some lunch?" She looked down at the wine glass I was holding and then up at me. Her face contorted in a confused expression.

The wine glass was the one I snatched from the bar the evening before. I slipped it into my purse as Liam escorted me past the table. When I arrived home, I sealed it in a ziplock plastic bag.

"We really need to talk about your drinking problem." I rolled my eyes at her. "You want to tell me what that is?" Daisy asked suspiciously.

"You know what it is," I said.

"I know I know what it is. Why do you have a wine glass at work?."

"I stole it from the bar last night." Daisy blinked at me.

"You did what?" She blinked again and pushed her glasses up her nose. "Is that the wine glass that man used last night?"

"The very one."

"And what are you planning on doing with it?" Daisy crossed her arms over her chest and leaned against the wall of my cubicle.

"I'm going to have it dusted for prints."

"But why? He was a jerk, but there's no law against being an asshole."

"It's probably nothing, but I just have one of those itchy feelings," I explained.

"The last time you had one of those itchy feelings we were arrested for trespassing." Daisy had that look that said she wasn't going along with another of my crazy ideas. Her eyes became hooded and took on a totally condescending expression that screamed her disapproval like a megaphone.

"That was different, and how was I supposed to know we were trespassing? The lock was off. That's practically an invitation," I defended. "And I got the company to drop the charges. Besides, I already told Lorie that I was bringing it by. She didn't blink an eye at the idea. Well, it was over the phone, but you know what I mean."

"Lorie, your college friend from the crime lab in Phoenix?" she asked, surprised.

"Yep. Want to drive to Phoenix with me?" I asked, smiling enthusiastically.

"Fine, but I think you're wasting your time. He was just a jerk of a guy with a big ego, and maybe a death wish. I wouldn't want to pick a fight with the McKenzie brothers, but maybe he was too stupid to know that," Daisy said.

"Then it's settled. You drive, and I'll buy lunch."

"You better be buying me lunch," Daisy grumbled.

Daisy left to get her things. The phone rang as I was slipping the glass into my purse. "Jessica Parker," I answered.

"Jess, it's Eric."

I sat up straighter in my chair and grabbed a pen and a slip of paper.

"Eric. How are you?" I hated doing the small talk when all I really wanted to know was the information.

"I'm good. I've got something for you, and it's pretty big," Eric said.

"I'm all ears."

"The campers both died from exsanguination."

"Ex-sang-u-what?" I asked. I knew I'd heard the term before but couldn't remember what it meant.

"They were drained of blood. They died from blood loss," Eric explained.

I was silent, trying to rationalize what he'd just told me.

"Jess?"

"I'm here. Sorry. Are you saying someone did this to them?" I asked.

"Yep. It's bizarre because there was little to no blood at the scene. But you can't quote me on that."

Daisy had grabbed her bag and returned to my cubicle. I motioned for her to wait a moment.

"That doesn't make any sense. Where would the blood have gone?" I asked.

"I'm not a detective, but it would seem to me that they must have been killed somewhere else, where the blood could have been drained or suctioned out, but that would be difficult to do. Then maybe they were taken back to their camp," Eric offered. "Pretty weird, huh?"

"That's an awful lot of work to murder two people. Why go to all that trouble with the blood?"

Daisy scrunched up her face.

"Crazy people do crazy things. I've got to run, but do you want to have dinner this week?"

Now it was my turn to scrunch up my face. "I'm sorry, Eric. My schedule is full this week. Let's talk next week," I offered, but was already thinking of ways to get out of it. This made me feel like a bad person, but at least if I met him next week for lunch, I could put the bug in his ear about Daisy. Sow the seeds and watch them grow.

"Oh. Okay, I'll call you then. Bye."

"Bye, Eric. And thank you for the information." I said, then ended the call.

I looked at Daisy. "Looks like Flagstaff has a double homicide," I said gravely.

Daisy mouthed the words *Wow,* just as Brenda Jeffrey walked up. "What's going on?" she asked. I eyed her from head to toe. Her perfect red glossy pumps matched her perfect red shiny lips, and it didn't help that her clothes were always designers that I couldn't afford even on clearance. If those stores had clearance racks.

I'd long suspected Brenda had a trust fund or a sugar-daddy in her pocket because we made similar salaries, and I could barely afford a manicure.

"Sorry, Brenda. We've got to run. Catch you later," I said, grabbing Daisy's arm and pulling her down the hall.

I did not need Brenda Jeffery sniffing around my story.

8

---

*L*iam

I could see Jessica in the rearview mirror as she stood in the street, watching me drive away. It felt so wrong to be moving away from her like this. Every nerve in my body, every thought in my mind wanted to be near her. But why? What was she to me?

I knew my words to her would obliterate any spark that may or may not have started from the kiss we shared the night before. Kissing Jessica was another mistake, and I needed to backpedal somehow. Leading her to believe it meant nothing to me was a necessary lie.

Allowing her to find me parked in front of her house was plain stupid. I managed to stay up most of the night, but at some point before dawn, I must have dozed off. I'd meant to be gone before she woke.

Kissing her had felt so good, so right. Not just physically, but almost, spiritually. I couldn't explain it. Where she was concerned, none of my emotions made any sense.

I couldn't let that happen again. Jessica Parker deserved

better than me. What woman could ever love the thing I was —the animal that I became?

If her response to my kiss was real, then I shouldn't have led either of us on. Not to mention being involved with her would be risky as hell, considering her profession. I should never forget her reasons for being with me last night. She's after a story. Her response to my kiss may have been a means to an end.

That thought bugged me. Why did I care if a beautiful woman wanted to use me for a story? There were worse things in life. But there was the crux of it—I did care. I knew nothing about Jessica, but my desire to keep her close, protect her, make love to her, was a physical ache.

I headed for the fire station and something that I knew and understood—work.

COLE AND SETH were at the station before me. That was a phenomenon that rarely, if ever, happened. The first thing I did was to head into the shower, then shave.

Seth gave me a knowing look when I passed him in the day room, and I knew he suspected that I'd spent the night with Jessica. I was close enough that if I focused hard, I could hear her breathing and knew the moment she drifted off to sleep. For a moment I'd imagined lying next to her, waking next to her, touching her. Basically, torturing myself.

Cole and Seth found me in the engine bay, double checking air tank levels. It was something to pass the time.

"So, you and the reporter, eh?" Cole asked jokingly.

"Nothing happened. I stayed in my truck to watch her house. We don't know what that thing was, and I didn't want to take a chance, so I stuck around," I said.

Neither Cole or Seth looked like they believed me. I didn't care.

"It's okay if something did happen. You don't need to feel bad about it," Cole said, trying to sound supportive.

"No, it's not. She's a reporter. What if she became curious and started digging into our past? Do you really want to move because I was attracted to a woman?" Cole looked surprised. "Seriously, Cole. Why do you think I left Harmony? I can't be with someone and have any level of real intimacy."

Cole's boyish demeanor changed. "You never should have left Harmony," Cole said, surprising me. Cole rarely lost his cool with anyone, so his words felt like a sucker punch.

"And why was that?" I asked, feeling my anger rising.

"Because you didn't give her the option to love you or leave you. You just left," Cole shot back.

In the past seven years, he'd never said a word about his opinion on the matter. I always knew he liked Harmony and even wanted us to marry, but I didn't realize that all this time, he thought I'd made a mistake.

"I left because it was the right thing to do. I left because Harmony deserved a normal life," I said.

"You left because you were scared she might reject you. You left so she couldn't leave you," Cole said. His face started turning red.

Seth stepped in the middle of us. "Whoa, you two. Let's take it down a notch." He turned toward Cole. "Cole, you're entitled to your opinion, but really, it was Liam's relationship and his call to make. He did what he thought was best. That's all any of us can do, right?"

Cole seemed to deflate a bit. He looked down for a few moments and then at me. "You're right. I'm sorry, Liam. What did I know? I was just a kid."

His apology eased my temper, but the guilt was nagging

at my heart. Was there some truth in Cole's perspective? I was angry because what he said hit a chord with me.

"Are you good, Liam?" Seth asked, turning to me.

"I'm as good as I can be," I said and reached my hand out to Cole. He looked at it, then grinning, pulled me into a rough hug.

"Okay, now that you two have worked out your issues, can we talk about that thing that came into the bar last night and what we should do about it?"

"Yeah, what the hell was that? He wasn't human, and he wasn't like us," Cole added.

"I'm not certain what he is, but I'm going to bet he's involved in the death of those two campers. That was either him or something like him that we smelled at the camp." I looked between Cole and Seth. "But I think I know who might have some information about him."

"Who?" Cole asked.

"Zoey." I watched Cole's eyes grow wide, while Seth let out a long whistle.

"Why do you think Zoey knows anything?" Cole demanded.

"Something she said to me last night," I said.

A call came in over the speakers. Fortunately, it was for the medics only. We paused our conversation as Dave and Tyler hustled past us to their truck to respond to the call.

"Someone better have lunch ready when we get back," Dave said before their truck pulled out of the bay.

"We're on it," Seth yelled.

Once again, we were alone to talk freely.

"And what did our little redheaded goddess say to you?" Seth prompted.

"It was more like a warning. She referred to him as a breed. She said, 'you don't need that breed of trouble.'"

Cole's eyebrows knitted together. "That sounds innocent

enough—like she was just warning you that he's a trouble-maker or something."

"No, there was more to it. She knows something. I'm going to ask her about it tomorrow," I said. "Let's get lunch going. Seth, maybe you can do one of your internet searches. See if shifters have any enemies or go to that *Dark Web* thing you do. Poke around in those weird forums."

"Those *weird forums* have given us more information about ourselves than we'd ever know otherwise. But, yeah, I'll do it," Seth said, turning to go into the station.

He had discovered that our condition is called Lyconism—shifter is the slang term used, as in shifting forms. Seth also heard that if we stayed in wolf form for an extended amount of time, we might not be able to change back. I didn't plan to test that theory. And although no one he'd communicated with had ever confessed to being a shifter, Seth suspected that some were.

———

THE NEXT MORNING, I was in the office waiting for the next crew to relieve us when Seth came to join me. "So, what's really going on with you and the reporter?"

"I told you, nothing," I said, not bothering to hide my annoyance with his question.

"Come on, Liam. This is me you're talking to. I know you, and you've been jumpy and short-tempered since she showed up on the mountain. What gives?"

Seth was always more intuitive than anyone gave him credit for. I leaned back in the chair and ran my hands through my hair. It was overdue for a trip to the barber. Finally, I looked at Seth.

"I don't know. It's weird. I don't know how to explain it. It's like I can barely contain my wolf when she's around." I watched Seth's reaction, trying to determine if he thought I was crazy or if my vague answer meant something to him. "Do you have any idea what I'm talking about? Does that make any sense to you?" I asked, honestly wanting to know.

Seth just stared hard at me. "No."

"Great. That's just great. I'm so glad we had this incredible bonding session, Seth." I started gathering some papers that needed to be filed.

"No, but I've read up on it," Seth said.

He had my attention. "What have you read?"

"Well, you know how wolves mate for life?"

"I don't like how this is starting, Seth," I warned.

"Just hear me out. Cole and I both noticed how you reacted to Jessica Parker. It was way out of character for you, big brother," Seth said.

"I'm not arguing that she isn't beautiful. I am a man." I crossed my arms over my chest.

"Yeah, but would you agree that you feel something for her beyond just physical attraction? Even though you know nothing about her?" Seth challenged.

"I can and have felt a lot of things when I've seen a gorgeous woman. You need to make your point fast, Seth."

"But this is different, isn't it? I'll bet that you haven't been able to think of much more. I'd even bet that you have an overwhelming desire to protect her—dare I add, make love to her." Seth leaned back and crossed his arms as if he'd made his point. He hadn't, but he was making sense even if I didn't want to admit it.

"Yeah. So?"

"She's the one you've connected with. I don't believe you have a choice in the matter. If what I've read is valid, and I believe it is, then you've already made the connection," Seth said, deadpan.

"But she's not like us. I can smell that she's human," I argued.

"Maybe not so ordinary, if she matched with you. Maybe somewhere in her DNA, she's got some wolf genes. I don't know. Maybe your perfect mate doesn't have to be a shifter. I didn't say I had all the answers."

The captain for the next shift walked into the office, ending our conversation, and leaving me with more questions about my feelings toward Jessica. And if Seth's theory has any truth to it, did she feel the same about me?

THE BURNING MOON opened by noon, but I knew Zoey didn't work days. At least, I'd never seen her there before six in the evening. So, I drove to the jiu-jitsu gym to grab a workout and maybe get some information on the two campers.

Several sheriff's deputies were members there and friendly acquaintances of mine. It was worth a shot, and I needed to burn some steam, anyway. Jessica's lips were on my mind, and I was having a difficult time concentrating on much else.

I found Rob Schaffer sparring with another man I didn't know. Tossing my bag on the bench, I started warming up with a jump rope while I watched them spar on the mat. Rob was shorter than me but built like a truck.

It took a good bit of supernatural strength for me to beat Rob when we sparred together, so he knew his techniques. He was also a deputy and might know something about the investigation. Sometimes this information would float around our small community of first responders, but if this proved to be a double homicide, the department would be more careful with what was shared.

When Rob's match was done, he shook hands and briefly hugged the other man before noticing me and walking over. He collapsed on the bench, breathing hard and dripping sweat.

"Good match, Schaffer," I offered.

"Thanks. How's it going, McKenzie?" he asked, still short of breath.

"Not bad. Heard anything about those campers we found?"

He laid his head back against the wall. "Weirdest shit. Would you believe they'd both been drained of blood? I'm not working that case, but what the hell."

I tried not to act overly interested since Rob's loose lips were giving me vital information I needed but didn't want to know. "That is weird. You ever seen anything like that?" I asked.

"Never, and I've seen some weird shit. Flagstaff has a murderer on the loose. Sort of makes my job in this sleepy town more exciting." Rob swatted me with the sweaty towel he'd just been using to dry off, then headed toward the showers before I could reply.

What the hell did this all mean? And what did that make the murderer?

Who am I kidding—I shifted into a big-ass wolf.

Of course, there are other things stranger than me. Six o'clock couldn't come fast enough. I needed to find out what Zoey knew and how she knew it.

9

*B*eaver Street Brewery was busy as usual. I sat at the bar and ordered a burger and beer. Whenever I ate alone at a restaurant, I'd listen to the conversations taking place around me and imagine myself in the role of the boyfriend, husband, or father.

My brothers were my family, and I thanked God for them, but on a human, elemental level, I longed for my own family. A wife, maybe some kids. Knowing I would never have that was something I'd come to accept. Remembering Seth's words about Jessica being my predestined mate had me imagining her by my side and what it would feel like to know I wasn't alone in this life. Maybe even a family with children. It almost felt real for a moment.

It was difficult to make it through a meal in a small town like Flagstaff, and not run into people you knew, but I managed to finish mine and pay without meeting anyone. I didn't even recognize the serving staff—only the bartender. There's something strangely comforting in knowing your bartender.

After dinner, I walked a couple of blocks over the train

tracks to the Burning Moon. It was early, and only a few regulars were having drinks. Zoey wasn't there yet, so I took a seat at the bar and ordered another beer.

I'd had another before she arrived for her shift. She spotted me at the bar and instantly stiffened. She knew what I'd come for or she had a strong suspicion. Her initial reaction to seeing me only convinced me more that she knew something.

I watched her grab a black apron and tie it around her hips. Zoey was an attractive woman, and now she had a bit of mystery floating around her. She'd worked here for only just over a month, but nobody seemed to know much about her.

It was apparent why Cole was so drawn to her. Her demeanor pulled you in, but her words pushed you away. Not that I'd tried, I could appreciate her beauty and personality, but she wasn't my type.

She greeted the other bartender, then walked over to me. I had a full beer, so I knew she came to talk.

"Hi, Liam."

"Hi, Zoey."

She placed both her forearms on the counter, leaning toward me a bit.

"You have questions for me."

"I do. You knew I would, didn't you?" I asked.

She stared at me for a moment. Her eyes darted behind me, then she said, "I'll be right there, Henry." To me, she said, "Hold tight."

Zoey walked out from behind the bar and over to the two men at the table in the corner—both locals I recognized. She spoke with them briefly then returned to draw two beers from the tap. Once she'd served them, she returned.

She leaned on the bar again. "I'll tell you what I can."

Meaning she wasn't going to tell me everything. "What do you know about that guy the other night?" I asked. I had to be careful. Let her do the talking without giving any of my secrets away. Cole could have been right, and I may have gotten the wrong idea about Zoey's comments.

"You don't know what he is?" she asked, cocking her head to the side. I didn't respond.

She raised her eyebrows. "I know he's a vampire, and that's all that matters."

I couldn't hide my surprise. So much for playing it cool. "Are we talking blood sucking vampires or someone who fancies themselves a creature of the night?" I asked, then took a sip of beer. Mostly, I was trying not to show ignorance in such matters. I was utterly floored, even if I shifted into a wolf several times a month.

"I think you know which one I'm speaking of." Surprisingly, she reached for my hand and held it while she closed her eyes for several seconds.

When her eyes opened, there was a softer look about them. She looked sympathetic—which made no sense. "I'm sorry. I thought you were playing games with me. You really don't know anything about it."

"How did you get that from touching me?" I asked, unnerved.

"Never mind that. All I can tell you is that he's a vampire. He's not that old, but still strong, and deadly." She searched my eyes. "He is your natural enemy. I think that much you sensed, right?"

I was suddenly on edge that if Zoey knew just from looking at the stranger that he was something unnatural, that she might know about me.

"Why do you say he's my natural enemy, Zoey?"

"Because your kind and his kind don't play nice," she said matter-of-factly.

I felt my hands go clammy, but I had to know. I glanced around the bar to be certain no one was within earshot.

"And what is my kind?" I asked, fearful that she knew, and yet hopeful that someone might be able to tell me more about myself.

"Do you want me to say it?" she challenged.

"Yes."

A long uncomfortable silence stretched. I didn't realize at first, but I was holding my breath.

"Wolf-shifter," she said, deadpan. "Or, a term from the old country would be a werewolf."

That was the first time I'd heard another person, besides my brothers, call it that. And I didn't know whether to pack up and leave town or breathe a sigh of relief.

"How do you know this?" I asked slowly.

"I've known it since the first night I served you here. How I know is not important. The fact that you're naïve about yourself and the potential threat the vampire presents is the issue. The vampire that came into the bar—you know—the one you started picking a fight with, can kill you. He's immortal, you're not. You may match him in strength, speed, but why risk it? Stay clear of him and maybe we'll get lucky. He could be passing through," Zoey said, as she began to wipe down the bar.

"What do you mean by *we'll get lucky?*"

"This is my home now. A vampire is a threat to us all. Just don't go looking for trouble." She walked away from me, and I knew she'd said all she was going to say.

I placed a hefty tip on the bar and stood up to leave. I walked to the door, feeling strange knowing she knew what we were. I stopped and turned around and walked back to her. She was busy wiping down the next table, but she looked up at me, a question in her green eyes.

"Why haven't you told anyone about our secret?"

She started wiping the table again. "You're not the only

ones with secrets in town, Liam. Now go watch over your pack—keep them safe."

She smiled and turned away.

I SENT a text to my brothers, asking them to meet me at the Weatherford Hotel, down the street from the Burning Moon. I didn't want to pressure Zoey any further and risk scaring her off.

We occasionally would meet at the bar upstairs that over-looked both Aspen Avenue and Leroux Street. It was another one of those businesses held over from another era. The hotel originally opened in 1900, and like most historic buildings, was said to house a few resident ghosts.

I'd never seen or heard any ghosts on the occasions I'd been there, but if I could magically change from man to beast, I supposed there was room for the possibility of ghosts. This thought didn't make me feel any less alone.

Within forty minutes, Seth and Cole entered the bar together. They spotted me sitting at a table and made their way over. I chose that spot because I liked to watch the nightlife down on the streets and in the bar. This position afforded me a view of both.

Seth sat down.

"I'll grab us a beer," Cole said, heading toward the bar.

"And a shot of tequila," Seth yelled. Cole gave him a thumbs up.

"You look like you've seen a ghost, big brother," Seth said, studying me.

"I wish. Ghosts might be simpler to handle."

Seth watched me, a concerned expression knitting his brows. It took a lot to ruffle Seth. At the very least he was a master at hiding his emotions. Cole always said that Seth felt more than any of us. Pa had said something like that to me, as well. I wasn't convinced that my devil-may-care brother was an emotional watershed underneath.

Cole returned carrying two beers.

"Where's the tequila?" Seth started to complain.

"It's coming." Cole had just sat down when a waitress came over carrying a small tray with three shots of tequila, a bowl of limes, and a salt shaker. I shook my head.

"Now we're talking," Seth said, as he set a shot glass in front of each of us and grabbed a lime wedge.

Cole did the same. It wasn't a tequila sort of gathering, but who was I to spoil the fun? I licked the back of my hand, sprinkled some salt where it was wet, and held a piece of lime with the same hand. With the other hand, I picked up the shot of tequila. I raised the glass in salute, then licked the salt, tossed the shot back, and quickly bit into the lime.

I knew my face looked like Cole and Seth's. Cole pounded the table, and Seth let out a loud war cry. A few of the patrons applauded and cheered. If neither of them started ordering more, we would be fine. We'd already figured out a long time ago that our DNA seemed to be resistant to intoxication. Meaning, it took three times the amount an ordinary man would need to get slobbering drunk. It wasn't difficult to get to the feel-good place, but anything else took way too much money and effort.

"I guess, after I tell you what I've learned, we'll appreciate those shots." I took a sip of my beer to wash the taste of tequila from my mouth.

"You talked to Zoey? What did she say?" Cole asked.

"Yeah, I did." I looked at each of them in turn. "She said that guy is a vampire, and that we would do good to stay clear."

"Like in the movies?" Seth asked, leaning forward.

Cole just stared at me like I'd sprouted another head.

"But real, I guess." I looked around the bar, wondering if the guy had left town or not. "There's more."

"Well, do tell. How can it get worse than that?" Seth said sarcastically.

I leaned closer, and Seth and Cole did the same. "I just heard that the two campers died of exsanguination."

Now both brothers sat back, slack-jawed and wide-eyed as they stared at me. Like me, they were no doubt trying to wrap their brains around the idea of vampires. It didn't make it any easier to believe in one freak of nature, just because we were…freaks, ourselves.

"You're shitting me," Seth said.

"It makes sense. He didn't smell like anything living. Hell, he smelled like death, only different." Cole was staring out the window, rubbing the stubble on his chin, deep in thought.

"And that same smell was at the campsite. It was him. That blood-sucking piece of shit killed those two people," Seth said.

Cole suddenly looked confused. "But how does Zoey know this?"

"Good question," I said. "She also knows what we are." I let that information sink in. If it wasn't such a dangerous situation, I'd loved to have a picture of the *oh, shit* looks on their faces. I still couldn't help cracking a smile.

"Aw, you're teasing," Cole said, leaning back and smiling too.

I just shook my head. He stopped smiling.

"Oh, crap! What are we going to do? Has she told anyone? How did she know?" Cole said, in his usual rush of energy that was difficult to keep up with. "Holy crap. Is she like us? Is she like him? Wait, no, she smells good but totally not like us."

Seth looked at me, and we both grinned and shook our heads.

"Slow down, Cole," Seth said.

"Let me try to unpack that. She isn't telling anyone. It might be that Zoey has her own secrets to protect. I don't know what they are, and I didn't push. The last thing I want to do is alienate her. She seems to be an ally, at this point," I said.

"Zoey knows," Cole said, mesmerized.

"But we don't know for certain if Zoey is a friend or foe," Seth said flatly.

"Of course, she's a friend," Cole said defensively.

"Seth's right, Cole. We don't know where Zoey stands in all of this. We need to remain cautious with her." I stared at Cole until he acknowledged my point. I knew he didn't agree, and it may have been possible he was now even more infatuated with Zoey.

10

JESSICA

Lorie Judd was a friend from college. We met freshman year when we lived in the same dorm while attending Arizona State University. She happened to study forensic science and turned out to be an excellent connection to have in my line of work.

She was the furthest thing from a rule follower and had no issues using the labs for an entirely personal request like pulling fingerprints from a wine glass that I pilfered from a bar. Lorie didn't even bother to ask me why.

"You're sure this is okay? It won't get you into any trouble?" I asked.

Lorie did her version of an eye roll. "We do this stuff all the time. What's one more set of fingerprints?" Lorie said while pulling on a pair of latex gloves.

Daisy looked at me, making her eyes wide. I smiled back at her smugly.

To Lorie, I said, "I really appreciate you doing this favor for me."

Lorie reached into the zip-lock bag and carefully pulled out the wine glass. She then placed it into a more official looking clear plastic bag that she had written on earlier.

"How soon will you have something for me?" I asked.

If the prints are clear, I'll have something for you this time tomorrow. If not, it can take several days and still come back empty." She peeled off the gloves and threw them into the trash.

"Where did you say this came from?"

I looked nervously at Daisy. "I didn't."

Lorie smiled at me. "Well, if this is someone who has been fingerprinted, you'll have a name. If not, you'll just have a fingerprint that won't tell you anything new."

"Actually, if the print isn't in the system, that will tell me something useful as well. So, anything you can give me will be great. Thanks again, Lorie," I said, handing her an envelope. It contained two tickets to a Phoenix Suns game with a VIP pass. I was given a few perks to utilize at my discretion. This seemed like a good trade.

"No problem," Lorie said, taking the envelope. "Always a pleasure doing business with you, Parker."

IT WAS a long quiet drive north to Flagstaff. Daisy liked to play her music loud, and since she was driving, I just went with it. Her favorite driving tunes consisted of the seventies and eighties rock.

I'd be hearing AC/DC's catchy tune "Back in Black" blaring in my head for days. I felt a bit guilty for not telling my parents that I was in Phoenix. I hadn't been to see them for over two months. And it wasn't like Flagstaff and Phoenix were all that far apart.

I didn't think Daisy would want to be dragged to the home I grew up in, and then sucked into staying for dinner. There was no such thing as a quick visit with my family.

The trip had wiped out the entire afternoon, being just over two hours' drive each way. It was after dark when Daisy pulled up in front of my house. "Thanks for going with me, even though it's most likely a waste of time," I admitted.

Daisy stayed in the car with the engine running. "No problem. I'll see you in the morning," she said, pushing the button to raise the window before driving away. She was a good sport and a good friend.

I went into my house and dropped my briefcase and coat on the living room chair, kicked off my heels, and went into the kitchen. My cell phone automatically synced with a small speaker that sat on the kitchen table. A pre-programmed station played classical music. I flipped on the lights as I walked into the kitchen.

I carried a soda and a piece of cold pizza from the fridge to the dining table. After eating half the pizza, I pulled my laptop from my briefcase and opened it on the table. Since I didn't have a desk, the kitchen table served dual purposes. It was typically scattered with papers and leftover dishes.

House cleaning wasn't one of my strengths. I promised myself that a housekeeper would be one of the first things I did once I landed a good enough job and I had some expendable income.

I'd been searching the web for Liam McKenzie and still hadn't found anything. Why had I even bothered? He didn't like me, that much was obvious. But boy, had that man crawled into my head. I was thankful that I had something else to work on. My next search was for exsanguination and its possible causes.

I called the sheriff's cell phone—I had him on speed dial. When he didn't answer, I left a message.

"Hi, it's Jessica Parker. A little bird told me that the deaths were ruled a homicide, and I'd like to get a statement from your department before I run an update to the story. Please call me back tonight or tomorrow morning. Thank you."

None of the search results seemed appropriate for the campers' cause of death or lack of blood. All the search results could still account for the missing blood.

Without knowing why, I typed the word *Vampire* into the *Google* search bar, then started laughing. *Keep it professional, Jess.*

I checked the time on the computer to see if I'd missed the nine o'clock news. I hadn't. It was 8:52, so I still had time.

There was a knock at the front door, which was odd for this time of night. I'd met a few people since moving to Flagstaff, and because I worked constantly, I hadn't met any of my neighbors. As I thought about it, this was the first time anyone had knocked at my door, besides the technician who set up my internet seven months ago and Daisy.

Maybe for that reason alone, the hairs on the back of my neck stood on end. That and the silly fact I'd typed *Vampire* into a search engine and already had some classic horror pictures on my laptop screen.

I took a quick sip of wine, grabbed my pepper spray from my purse and made sure it was in the *ON* position. There was no spyglass in the door because the house I rented was at least seventy years old, and looked like it had never been replaced.

I looked out the front window but didn't spot any unfamiliar cars. My curiosity got the best of me and I opened the door, instantly regretting my decision.

The man from the bar stood on my front porch. It was all I could do not to slam the door in his face. He was, even more, striking up close, which still did nothing to calm my racing heart. *What was he doing at my house?*

"Yes?" I asked, afraid to say much more and let him know how much his appearance had rattled me.

"Jessica Parker." The way he said my name was like a physical caress over my skin. I had to force down a shiver. All my warning bells were sounding, but the reporter in me was beyond curious why he was here. *That was what killed the cat, wasn't it?*

Suddenly, my wits seemed to show up, along with some attitude. "You know my name, but I don't know yours or why you're at my home." I think my fear made my words sound even ruder than I'd meant them to.

The look in his eyes did not match the tone of his words. "Forgive me. My name is Lorenzo, and I came to apologize if my behavior offended you the other evening. It was not my intention, I assure you."

My pepper spray was hidden behind the door. "How do you know where to find me?"

He smiled then, and it was the most predatory look I'd ever seen. "Bradley, the intern at KUTV, was kind enough to share your address with me when I told him why I needed it. I hope you don't mind."

If he had mentioned anyone at the station beside Bradley, I wouldn't have believed him. Nobody at work would have shared my private address without my permission, except maybe Bradley, our eighteen-year-old intern.

Bradley was a hard worker, and way too sweet for the profession he aspired to. He was also naïve and extremely gullible—even more reasons he'd chosen poorly for his career. News reporters were none of those.

I rolled my eyes without thinking. "Bradley shouldn't have given out my address, and a phone call would have been more appropriate." I made certain that he could detect my annoyance.

"I must apologize. I've upset you again," Lorenzo said. His slight accent was at times difficult to detect at all. I suspected he'd spent more of his life in America than he had in the country he'd acquired the accent.

"Fine, apology accepted. Good night, Lorenzo." I started to close the door, but a highly polished boot blocked it. I looked from his boot up into his multifaceted blue eyes and just stared. That would have been a good time to use the pepper spray, but instead, I found that I couldn't stop looking into his eyes.

"I'd like to take you to dinner to make up for my rude behavior toward your…friends. Will you allow me?" he asked, leaning toward me.

Normally, this is where my fight or flight mode might engage. Normally, this is where I'd seriously consider using the pepper spray that hung limply in my hand. Normally, I'd find everything about this situation to be weird and profoundly creepy.

Normally.

Instead, my mouth warred with my will. I wanted to tell him to take his scary-self off my rented property. What I actually said—and this was a battle of epic proportions —was, "No."

Not, *get lost, go screw yourself…*just *no*. That was the only thought I could get to reach my almost useless lips. I was surprised I managed that much. My mind was screaming at me to say *yes*. It was the weirdest thing. It felt like I wanted to do anything he asked of me—which, somewhere deep in my mind I knew I didn't want to do.

I was surprised, but so was he. His perfectly shaped dark brows came together in concentration as he continued to hold my gaze captive.

"I must insist, " he said firmly. Gone was the friendly pretense.

Again, it was like a battle raging inside me. I knew I needed to say *no*, but I desperately wanted to say *yes*. Like, wanted it *bad*.

"No," was all I could say, and it came out like a soft whisper, or maybe a whimper. We stood there, staring at one another. That was the last thing I remembered before I found myself staring at an empty porch.

I looked around at the dark yard and wondered if I'd imagined the entire thing. Then I looked at the pepper spray in my hand and down at the clothes I was still wearing. Shaking my head to clear it, I locked the door and walked back to my computer. The screen saver was bouncing smiley-faces all over the screen, which was odd.

My screen-saver was set to start after an hour of no activity on the computer. I looked at the clock on the screen and gasped. It was ten o'clock. I checked the clock on the microwave just to be sure. Sure enough, I'd somehow, lost an hour of time.

1

I HAD the strangest dreams that night. It occurred to me that I could have had some sort of psychological episode brought on by stress, or heaven forbid, a brain tumor. Those were the restless thoughts floating around my mind when I finally did manage to fall asleep.

The entire night I dreamed of Lorenzo's eyes that could make me do anything he wanted me to. But there was another element that made no sense at all. An unusually large wolf with tan fur and glowing amber eyes kept appearing. And then it was the wolf's eyes that watched me.

By the end of each seemingly random dream, Liam was the one kissing me. That was the only good thing I remembered. Why couldn't all the dreams have starred the sexy fire captain? In my dreams, he wasn't the sort of a jerk who blew hot and then cold.

I awoke that morning, not entirely sure if some or all of

the previous evening was real or part of an elaborate dream. When Daisy picked me up for work, I didn't mention my strange night. What could I say that didn't make me sound crazy? I felt strongly that Lorenzo came to my house. That was too clear not to have happened. It was what I couldn't remember that worried me.

Daisy handed me a coffee from our favorite local roaster, and I smiled my gratitude at her as I reverently curled my hands around the paper cup.

I didn't want to worry Daisy. For all her efforts at feigning a laid-back Flagstaff attitude, she had a tendency to be a worrier. She offered me three different holistic remedies whenever I complained of a headache.

I had a drawer full of special teas, supplements, and dried herbs she'd given me over the last six months. I always thanked her then secretly popped a Tylenol. Daisy meant well.

"You don't look like you slept a wink. Maybe you should put some concealer under your eyes before we film your segment this morning," Daisy said, stealing a glance at me.

"Gee, thanks," I said sarcastically.

"Sorry. I was strictly speaking to your professional side. You know, from the other side of the lens," she said, smirking.

"I know. I didn't sleep well last night," I said, already lowering the vanity mirror on the passenger side. I pulled a thick makeup pencil from my bag and dabbed concealer over my dark-ringed eyes.

"Better?" I asked, turning toward her.

If you were a professional who worked in front of a camera at a moment's notice, there were certain essentials that you carried at all times. One was a small stash of makeup, and two was a hair-tie for windy weather or bad hair days. I kept a dress jacket hanging in my cubicle and another in my car that I could throw over just about any top and be camera ready from the waist up in under three minutes. *Tricks of the trade.*

She glanced at me. "Sure." Daisy didn't sound convincing, but I was too tired to care this morning. Too many thoughts going through my sleepy brain.

———————

THE SHERIFF RETURNED my call shortly after I arrived at the station.

"Ms. Parker, I don't know where you received your information about the victims, but that is not the official statement from the department. This matter is still under investigation." The sheriff's voice kept breaking up, but I could tell he wasn't happy with me.

"My sources are solid. Are you sure you wouldn't like to make an official statement?" I asked. Sometimes the authorities liked to sit on information longer than necessary. A bit of prompting went a long way to move the process along.

There was a long silence on the phone, and I started to wonder if we'd been cut off before he spoke. "We do not have an official statement at this time, and I would encourage you not to spark fear within the community by reporting carelessly."

It was the sheriff's turn to try to get under my skin. I was ready for it. "Sheriff, you and I both know this was not accidental or natural. That means this is a double homicide. Unless you can give me a good reason why I shouldn't warn the public that there is potentially a predator walking among us, then I'm running the story."

Again, silence.

"You do what you feel is right. I'll do what I know is right. Good day, Ms. Parker," he said before the line went dead.

Okay, his last jab did get to me a bit. But I knew that as a citizen in this community, I'd want to know. It was my responsibility to inform the community, especially about something so important.

Also, the campers deserve to have their story told, and I was the person to get it done. There was some guilt on my part that this story could get me the recognition needed to land me a better job in a bigger city. That was my number one goal, but every time I thought about it, I felt unsatisfied. The thought of moving away and never seeing Liam again added to my troubled thoughts. He didn't like me and I knew nothing about the man, so it shouldn't have been a consideration.

Surprisingly, Flagstaff had grown on me. I'd started hiking once a week with Daisy. It was a beautiful place to live, and I recognized the appeal. But, I'd been planning my dream job since high school, and Flagstaff didn't fit the image I'd come up with.

Painting helped me cope with negative feelings whenever I'd get stressed while focusing on my goals and plans. But sometimes I wondered if they were really my goals.

I WANTED to shoot the scene just as the sun was setting, with the forest behind me for dramatic effect. We'd have to drive thirty minutes there and back, but I felt it was worth it.

I managed to convince my boss to let me air the story on the nine o'clock news. With barely enough time to catch the sunset, Daisy and I were on our way to the trailhead to shoot the report. The sun had just dipped below the tree line, and the sky was breathtaking. A part of me wanted to just sit on the side of the road and enjoy it.

My professional side wanted that sunset and the forest as

the backdrop for our report. Daisy and I stared at the sky a moment longer, then got busy setting up. I went over my notes and key points, and Daisy set up her camera and lights, then played with the exposure.

We were ready to roll when my phone rang. I'd forgotten to silence it, which happened more than I like to admit. I began fishing it out of my jacket pocket, and Daisy rolled her eyes.

"This is Jessica Parker."

"Jess, it's Lorie."

"Hey, Lorie! Can I call you right back? We're trying to shoot a story, and I'm losing my sunset."

"Forget the sunset. I've got a question for you. How the hell did you get that glass? Better yet, where did you get that glass?" Lorie demanded.

The seriousness of her voice caught me off guard. "What...what do you mean?" I stammered, as I put her on speaker phone so Daisy could hear.

"Those prints belong to a dead guy."

Silence ensued as Daisy and I stared blankly at each other, the beautiful sunset was forgotten.

"That's impossible. He was fully alive when he drank the wine," I said, my mind racing, trying to make sense out of what she was saying.

"There were only three sets of prints on the glass. Yours, a woman named Zoey Espinoza, and a hitman from the Italian mafia named Lorenzo Romano," Lorie said, sounding edgy. "What have you got me into, Parker?"

I blinked several times at Daisy, whose eyes were huge behind her black-rimmed glasses. As the sun was setting and the sky was growing dimmer, Daisy began peering into the trees nervously.

"That's completely impossible. You must have mixed up the prints. Did you speak to the person who did the test?" I asked, thinking of logical ways a dead man's prints could be associated with the wine glass that I'd supplied. The only explanation was an error.

"I ran the test, Jess. There were no mistakes, and the prints were perfect and clear. Now, I'll ask one more time, and then I'm walking away. Where did you get this glass?" Lorie asked.

"Are you in trouble for doing this for me?" I asked cautiously.

"I have a friend in IT, he's waiting for a phone call from me, and if I give him the word, he's going to delete that this request ever went through the system, hopefully before someone notices the hit."

I let out a breath I hadn't realized I'd been holding. "If you're certain there were no mistakes made, then why don't you call your friend? I'll try to figure this out on my end," I suggested.

There was a pause. "Fine. Whatever you're involved in, you should walk away," Lorie said. "This guy was bad news when he was alive, and anything to do with him is nothing you want to be involved with."

"Thanks for the advice and the help, Lorie." I thought for a moment. "When did he die?" I asked, mostly out of curiosity.

"Over twenty years ago. He was found murdered, most likely a professional hit. He was pronounced dead by the coroner's office in New York City, but his body was stolen from the morgue and never recovered."

That was all Daisy needed to hear. She was packing up her equipment with the speed of a squirrel on crack. I waved at her to hold off. We still had to film with or without the lovely sunset. Daisy shot me a pained look but stopped her frantic task.

"Well, that's an interesting, yet creepy detail. How old was Lorenzo when he was murdered?" I asked.

"Um…looks like the death certificate says twenty-eight."

"I'm curious why Zoey's prints were in the system," I asked, mostly thinking out loud.

"She was arrested for a domestic disturbance in Tucson last year. Be safe, Parker," Lorie said before the call went dead.

Domestic disturbance, huh? I wondered what Zoey's story was.

Daisy was standing nervously beside the tripod she set up for the second time that evening. There was hardly any light left in the sky.

"Daisy, relax. I know how it sounded, but let's get real. People don't come back from the dead. There has to be a logical explanation. I'll talk to Zoey. Maybe she can shine some light on this—give us something we haven't considered yet." I held the microphone, waiting for her to agree.

"I don't like this, Jess. That was too weird. And he totally looked Italian!" Daisy exclaimed.

"Yeah, but—"

"Tell me he didn't look like a Lorenzo Romano?" she demanded. I knew if I told her that the guy came to my home and said his name was Lorenzo Romano, we'd never get our segment filmed and she might even pack up and leave town. Not that the thought hadn't crossed my mind when Lorie said that name.

"Okay, in a totally stereotypical way, yes," I admitted. "But Daisy, come on. Are you even going to try to assume he came back from the dead, didn't age a bit—because that man wasn't a day past thirty—then drank a glass of wine while picking a fight with the McKenzies?"

I saw the moment that Daisy realized how crazy her suspicious thoughts were. She laughed nervously, but still glanced around one more time. I smiled back at her and raised my mic as if preparing to be filmed. "Ready?" I asked, feeling a tiny bit guilty for not giving Daisy all the information.

She smiled sheepishly at me then moved behind the lens. "Ready," she replied. She held up her fingers to silently countdown from three.

Three, two, one...

A bright light shone in my eyes, but I kept my face completely neutral as if I wouldn't be completely blind by the time Daisy killed the lights.

"This is Jessica Parker with KUTV News at Nine, with an important update regarding the two campers found dead just four nights ago..."

$\mathcal{L}$iam

After several tequila shots and a few beer chasers, Seth, Cole, and I were feeling good.

"So, do we leave that creep alone or send him packing?" Cole asked.

"I say an eye for an eye," Seth said in a cheery tone that didn't match what he was implying.

"If he's what Zoey said he is, he's already dead. I think we need more answers from our red-headed bartender," I said. College basketball was playing on a couple of the televisions hanging above the L-shaped bar. Another was playing a local station but was on commercials at that moment.

It was a few minutes before nine o'clock, and I found myself glancing at the screen that would be showing the local news. Jessica worked for KUTV, and it was almost a given that she'd be seen reporting on something happening around town. Sometimes, she'd do reports in neighboring Sedona, Phoenix, and occasionally Tucson.

Seth noticed that I was distracted. Leaning back in his chair, he grinned at me. "Waiting for your girl to show up on the nightly news, Liam?" Seth teased. I shot him an annoyed look, hoping he'd drop it.

I didn't want to believe his soul-mate or fated-mate idea about Jessica and me, but I also couldn't ignore my feelings for her. It wasn't normal in any way, but yet, it felt so natural. It was my head that refused to accept this explanation, even if deep down I wanted it to be her.

Seeing my discomfort, Cole joined Seth as they watched me with wide grins as if they had me all figured out. "Big brother's got a crush. And here I thought you'd be a lonely old bachelor."

Watching them leaning back in their chairs with their arms crossed over their chests made me want to teach them both a lesson. I linked my foot around Cole's chair leg and pulled. Cole crashed down onto the floor of the bar, but Seth was too fast for me. He sat his chair down before I could do the same to him.

"Okay, okay," Cole laughed from his prone position on the floor.

Laughing, I reached down to help Cole up. The bar had filled up since we'd arrived and we had drawn the attention of just about everyone there. Once they saw that we were laughing, even Cole, they began to lose interest, and slowly went back to their drinks and conversations.

"Back to the topic. I think we need to find this…" I leaned forward and lowered my voice. "…vamp and tell him to get the hell out of town."

"I'll go along with that, but how do we find him?" Seth asked.

"Well, we know he goes to bars. I think that's where he first met or saw the two campers. Remember the matchbook at the campsite? We know that the vamp and the campers had the Burning Moon in common," I said.

"Flagstaff has more bars than fast food joints. Do we go

bar hopping every night and hope we don't become alcoholics before we find him?" Seth complained, then signaled the waitress for another round.

"I thought you'd love this idea, Seth. Won't you feel right at home?" Cole teased, and I laughed. Seth ignored Cole's comment completely.

"I think it will be best if we divide and conquer. Each night we split and go to three different bars from nine to eleven. That's when the vamp arrived at the Moon the other night," I said.

"What do we do if we see him?" Cole asked.

"Call in the reinforcements," I said, slapping Seth's shoulder. "We can get to just about anywhere in town in under five minutes."

"That could work," Seth said. The waitress brought three more draft beers and set them on the table. Seth gave her a smile and a five-dollar tip. She beamed at him and went back to the bar. Seth had that effect on most women. Don't know what happened to Cole and me. Maybe we just didn't work it like he did. I think I still remembered how to flirt.

"Let's do it. We can start tomorrow night since we're off shift the next few days," Cole said, with his usual enthusiasm.

"Maybe we should talk to Zoey one more time before we confront this guy," Seth said. I put my finger to my lips and stared at the television above the bar.

Cole and Seth followed me as I moved to the bar. "Turn that up, please," I asked the bartender. He stopped wiping down the glass he was holding to pick up a remote and point it at the television.

The news channel was showing the faces of the two campers. Below their smiling faces were the names, Chance Riggs and Becca Ford.

"KUTV reporter, Jessica Parker has a special update

regarding the two hikers, now identified as…" a male voice was saying.

Jessica, standing in front of a wooded area, appeared on the screen. The shot showed her from the waist up, holding a microphone. Her face was serious as she struggled to keep the strands of her blonde hair from blowing across her face.

"This is Jessica Parker with KUTV News at Nine, with an important update regarding the two campers found dead just four nights ago in a remote area of the Coconino National Forest. The two hikers have been identified as twenty-seven-year-old Chance Riggs of Las Vegas, Nevada, and his girlfriend, twenty-five-year-old Becca Ford, also of Las Vegas. Their families have been notified, and their deaths are still under investigation by the Coconino County Sheriff's Department." Jessica continued to struggle with the wind in her hair.

So, the campers now had names. It helped to humanize them. We'd been referring to them as the campers for so long, but they were people who lost their futures to a monster.

My gaze stayed glued to Jessica's face. It was difficult to tell exactly where she was, but I had an awful feeling it was the same area where the camp…Chance and Becca were found.

"KUTV has it under good authority that their deaths will be ruled as homicides, although the sheriff's department is not willing to confirm this information at this time. Both victims were reported to be missing most of their blood, but puncture marks along the carotid artery of each victim were the only injuries found. The wounds on the necks of the victims are assumed to be where the blood loss originated from." Jessica seemed to pause to collect her thoughts and refer to a small notepad she held in her other hand.

Seth, Cole, and I shared anxious glances with each other before turning back to the screen.

"After speaking with Special Agent Bethany Lancaster with the FBI in Cleveland, Ohio, we've learned that vampirism is actually a mental condition that some individuals believe they have. The news show *Twenty-Twenty* aired a report about an entire underground society that spans the globe. While many of these self-proclaimed vampires also claim to despise harming others, questions still arise. Could Vampirism be a factor in these murders? From Coconino National Forest and KUTV News, this is Jessica Parker, saying goodnight, and be safe, Flagstaff."

The program switched to a commercial, and I looked at my brothers. "I have to warn her. She has no idea what she's doing." I ran my hands through my hair and moved to leave. I needed to find Jessica.

Seth stood in my way and put his hands on my shoulders. "What are you going to tell her, Liam? Stop and think about this. We don't really know what Zoey is hiding—"

"Stop talking about her like that. She's not our enemy, or she wouldn't have warned Liam," Cole interrupted, looking agitated.

"Just because you have a high school crush on the woman doesn't mean she's not hiding something," Seth said to Cole.

"Maybe I can make her understand that she's drawing too much attention to herself. I don't plan to tell her our secrets, Seth," I said, pushing his hands away.

"Okay, okay. Let's all go talk to Zoey and then you can check on your girl," Seth suggested. "Wait a minute." Seth turned to the bar to settle our tab, and Cole and I grabbed our jackets from the coat rack. Seth walked over, and I handed him his coat. We left the upstairs bar and walked down the stairs and through the lobby filled with students, locals, and a few visiting parents.

We made our way down the street to the Burning Moon. I didn't even have Jessica's number. What an idiot I was. So busy keeping her at arm's length that I never asked for her phone number. No wonder she glared after me when I drove away that morning.

We crossed the street, and I walked into the Burning Moon for the second time that evening. I scanned the now full bar for any sign of the vampire but didn't see him. Zoey caught my eye and pointed to the small television screen above the bar. Then she shook her head. She must have seen Jessica's report as well.

We walked up to the bar and sat down in the last three empty seats. For appearance's sake, I'd order three more beers. It was a good thing we were shifters, or we'd be falling all over the place by now.

Zoey came to take our order but didn't look receptive to talking. Her body language was stiff and formal.

"Three drafts, Zoey," I said.

"Please," Cole added shyly. Zoey paused and looked at Cole, then rewarded him with a warm smile.

Cole suddenly looked like we hadn't been talking about vampires and shit all night. The smile on his face was infectious. I found myself smiling too.

When Zoey returned with our beers, I asked, "Can we talk to you?"

She hesitated. It was a busy night, so there were two bartenders working. Zoey looked around the bar. Then she said, "Give me a minute."

She took several orders, served the drinks, filled several baskets with peanuts and small pretzels, then said something to the other bartender. He continued drawing a mug of beer but nodded his head. She wiped her hands on her black apron and nodded for us to join her as she walked to the door by the bathrooms marked Employees Only.

We followed her inside. Zoey stopped in the hall. When the door closed, it muffled out most of the noise from the crowded bar.

"I only have a minute. What your girl did was not good, Liam," Zoey said, her green eyes flashing.

"Would everyone stop calling Jessica Parker my girl. I just met her," I said. Zoey raised her eyebrows at me as if I'd just lied about having my hand in the cookie jar.

"What do you guys want from me? I've already told you more than I should have," Zoey said, crossing her arms over her chest.

"Yeah, why did you say anything? Why do you care?" Seth asked, leaning his arm on the wall above her head. He didn't seem to ruffle her feathers in the least. She just gave Seth an annoyed look.

"Because you three seem pretty clueless and I didn't want to see you get hurt. Maybe I'm a nice person," she said with a look that dared Seth to argue with her.

Luckily, he didn't. "How do you know about vampires or…us?" I asked.

She looked angry now. "That's not your concern. Next question. The clock is running."

"How can we stop him?" Cole asked. Zoey's face softened when she looked at Cole.

"I don't know that you can. My best advice is to stay away. And I'd keep an eye on your girlfriend. She stepped in it big-time tonight. Vampires are a touchy bunch. She practically accused them of having a mental disorder." Zoey touched Cole's arm as she slipped past him to return to the bar.

Cole, Seth, and I stood in the empty hall, holding our now warm beers, and said nothing for a few moments. Then Seth broke the silence.

"We can't let him come here and murder people. He needs to go, or we don't deserve to call this place home."

"I agree. I don't think we can sit back knowing he killed those two people, while we hope the big bad vampire leaves town," I said.

"Then it's settled. We'll stake out the bars tomorrow night. If we find him, we'll escort his designer ass out of town," Cole said, still bouncing from one foot to the other. Sometimes his energy was a good thing, and other times, like now, it put me on edge.

I looked at my brothers, both deep in their own thoughts, and I worried for the first time about their safety and all the wrong ways that this situation could play out.

For the first time in years, I was unsure if I was doing the right thing or not. The fork in the road had no clear direction.

12

I said goodnight to Cole and Seth, then drove to Jessica's house. I wanted to see that she was safe and somehow warn her about the danger without telling her how crazy it really was or exposing myself in the process.

But underneath all the excuses, I knew that I needed to see her, be near her—to touch her. On the surface, she was the worst person I could have been insanely attracted to. Her profession alone meant the risk was tenfold.

Jessica didn't even seem like my type, but seriously I had nothing to compare to, besides Harmony. Jessica Parker appeared to be career driven, obsessed with following a story, and fiercely independent. I respected these characteristics but felt less than adequate to be a part of her world.

What did I have to offer a woman like that? I'd only ever been a small-town firefighter, and I suspected she had big plans that did not include a guy like me. And that's pretending that I don't have a secret so big, she'd either exploit it for a sensational story or run screaming. Or maybe both.

Her front porch light was on, but the house was dark.

Since it was still early, I parked my truck on the street and waited.

―――――

Thirty minutes later, a slick looking BMW pulled into her drive, and Jessica stepped out, carrying a briefcase, a purse, and what looked to be a stack of books. The driver did not get out of the car. Instead, they backed out of the drive and drove off before Jessica had even reached the door of her house.

I got out of my truck and walked across the lawn. Not wanting to frighten her, I made a coughing sound. She jumped and let out a high-pitched squeak anyway, but I didn't expect her to spin around and threaten me with pepper-spray.

"Woah! Sorry, don't shoot," I said, still worried she might press that button.

She looked horrified when she recognized me. Letting out a long-exaggerated sigh, she slumped and leaned against the front door. "I almost sprayed you in the face. What are you doing sneaking up on me like that, Captain McKenzie?" she asked, emphasizing the formal title.

I smiled. "I guess I deserve that. I'm sorry about the other morning. And I'm sorry for startling you just now." I reached for the pile of books, and she let me take them from her.

"Fine. Apology accepted. Now, would you like to come in and tell me why you're here? I've had a rough day, and I could use a drink." When I nodded, she turned around and finished unlocking the door.

She walked in and I followed her, looking around before turning to close the door. The house was old and needed some work. I assumed she was renting. The sparse furnishings were more modern but somehow made the space feel warm and inviting. I also felt like a bull in a china shop. The room was covered in light pink and brown colors, and certainly had a feminine feel to it.

There were frameless paintings on canvas that covered just about every inch of wall space. Many were nature scenes such as forests, streams, mountains, or the ocean. Some were portraits of different individuals with somber, smiling, or laughing faces.

At first, I thought she must collect art. But then I saw a painting of a white wolf with a forest in the background. The wolf seemed to be the focus of the picture. I leaned forward to read the artists name—J. Parker.

Most of the art was by J. Parker. As I studied the paintings more closely, I saw a theme in many of the nature scenes. A light-colored wolf appeared in random places, almost as an intentional signature. I could feel my heart thumping in my chest as my wolf responded.

Jessica didn't seem to notice me inspecting the art on her walls. I placed the books on the small kitchen table that must have doubled as her desk. It was covered with papers, markers, notebooks, and an iPad. The pizza box looked out of place. I'd guessed her to be a healthy eater.

Many women thought they had to starve themselves to look good, but I preferred natural curves, like Jessica's.

Shaking my head to clear the thoughts that had already crossed my mind, I stood next to the table feeling awkward. This was a new thing for me. I liked being in charge and in control. This was like walking into a minefield. Every step was a risk.

Jessica had disappeared around the corner, which I could tell was the kitchen because of the small amount of counter and cabinets that I could see. I planned to ask her if she was the artist. Maybe it was a family member.

Jessica came out of the kitchen a minute later carrying

two well-filled wine glasses and offered me one. I hesitated for a moment, but then took the drink from her.

She smiled a weak smile and walked over to the couch, where she tucked her legs under her and motioned for me to take the chair next to her. "Sit, relax. Lord knows I need to," she said, taking a long sip of red wine.

I'd already managed to drink enough to feel good. What was one more if it made her happy? Drinking alone sucked. I took a sip and realized it was good. I'd never been much of a wine drinker, preferring beer or whiskey.

"Who's the artist?" I asked, motioning around the room.

"Do you like them?"

"They're incredible," I said honestly.

"I painted these. I have many more in the spare room," she said, getting up. "Would you like to see?" she asked shyly.

"Yes." I followed her down a short hallway and into a small room. Jessica flipped on the light, and I almost dropped the glass of wine. The room looked like an artist's studio with paintings covering the walls, an easel, and a small table covered in trays, with globs of dried paint, and many tubes of paint that resembled toothpaste.

But those things I almost expected. The pictures themselves were what took my breath away and made my stomach clench. Every single painting or sketch featured a wolf or wolves. Many were white, or tan, but others were grey, brown, or black.

I couldn't stop staring at the paintings. When I finally looked at Jessica, she seemed embarrassed. "I know. It's a little obsessive, isn't it? You should know that painting is therapy for me. It relaxes me, makes me happy. You know, a healthy hobby," she said, looking around.

"Why do you paint so many wolves?" I could barely manage to ask.

"I don't know. I love them. They're beautiful to me. But

97

mostly, because I've been dreaming of wolves since I was a child. I don't know why. I just do. Did you know that wolves mate for life?" she asked innocently.

"Yes, I do…know that," I stammered as she moved past me and switched off the light.

I didn't know what to say or what to think, so I followed her back into the living room, shocked into silence for the moment.

"Why are you here, Liam?" Jessica asked, looking tired.

"Why don't you tell me why you need a drink." I wanted to know what had upset her, but I was still trying to calm my racing heart and mind.

She studied me a moment. "Okay, I'll share. That was my boss who dropped me off. Daisy was my ride, but she went home hours ago, while I stayed to have my ass chewed," she said, then took another sip of wine.

"Why was your boss mad?" I asked, truly curious, and maybe deep-down thinking how I'd like to beat the crap out of anyone who gave her a bad day. These sorts of thoughts were messing with my mind. And now the paintings. What was happening here? Was Seth right about Jess and me?

"Did you see the news tonight?" she asked. I nodded. "Well, Mr. Boss, that's what we call him, approved the report, but when he got heat from the mayor and the sheriff, he needed a scapegoat, so…" she trailed off, holding her wine with one hand and absently toying with the ends of her long blonde hair with the other.

She was turning me on and didn't even have a clue. It was so bad that I couldn't ignore Seth's suggestion about her being my perfect mate. I didn't buy it entirely, but the signs were beginning to overwhelm me.

"I take it they didn't like what you implied?" I asked.

She laughed, but it was a bitter sound. "Seems like I may

have ended my career before it ever really started. Might not be the worst thing."

I wondered what she meant by that. "I'm sorry," I said. And I was.

She looked at me strangely, like she was trying to figure something out. "Your turn. Why are you here?"

I took a deep breath and exhaled. "I'm here because I saw your story. I came to ask you to drop it. There are things happening that could get you hurt," I said, leaning forward and resting my forearms on my knees.

"What do you know that I don't, Liam?" She set her wine on the table and mirrored my position. Our faces were so close I could smell her perfume and her scent under that. She held my gaze, waiting for my reply.

"Just enough to know that you may be in danger. Some of it's just a gut feeling, but…" I said, looking away from her intense gaze.

"And why do you care?" she asked. That was the million-dollar question.

"Maybe I'm a good person and don't want to see a beautiful woman get hurt," I offered. Twelve inches was all that separated us.

"You think I'm beautiful?" she whispered. I was fighting to keep my wolf in check. All I could do was nod.

Jessica's gaze dropped to my lips, and before I knew what she was doing, she'd slid from the edge of the sofa, taking my head in her hands, and kissed me long and hard. She tasted so good.

My arms slid around her and pulled her up with me as I stood, never breaking our connection. She melted to me like a second skin, and I knew there was something there. Nobody, not even Harmony, had ever felt like this. Jessica was a need, as essential as breathing. But what was I supposed to do about it?

I pulled back, and she seemed to compose herself a bit. I wondered if she regretted her bold move. I still held her arms, but she let her hands slide back down to her sides. "I'm sorry. I think the stress, the murders, and the dreams must be affecting me more than I realized. I don't normally act like this," she said, looking embarrassed. "I'm attracted to you, and maybe it's just that I haven't dated in over a year, or maybe it's the situation—" I silenced her words with my lips.

I'd heard enough to know that she felt something for me like I did for her. Maybe not exactly like me, but it was something to hold onto.

"I…can't get…involved with anyone…" she breathed in between kisses.

"Me…either," I said, letting my lips travel down her neck.

Her head fell back, and I moved my fingers through her hair and held her head in that position while I continued my path down along her collarbone and back up her neck to claim her lips again. My wolf kept saying, *mine*, inside my head.

She pulled back and placed her palms on my chest to stop me when I would have continued. "Stop. I can't. I mean, I don't have casual sex. It's a rule for me," she said, looking conflicted.

I didn't want to stop, but I was glad she had the willpower to pull the brakes because I had none now. She'd removed my carefully constructed control with a single kiss.

"It's okay. I don't want casual sex with you," I said, grinning mischievously. I watched her face as she tried to figure out what I'd meant, exactly. Then she smiled back shyly. She moved away from me then.

I reluctantly released her and returned to my chair. Jessica went back to her place on the sofa. I sipped the wine in the awkward silence that followed our brief encounter.

"So, are you going to tell me why you think I'm in danger? Or will I have to force it out of you?" she joked.

I watched her for a moment, my thoughts serious once again. "I don't believe those campers died in a natural way," I said, watching her expression.

"Murder isn't natural, Liam."

"It may not be a natural way to die, but it's an expected part of human history. One of the first sons of man killed his brother. It happens," I offered, settling into the chair and throwing one arm around the back.

"So, what are you saying?"

What am I saying? "That the murderer isn't human."

"I don't believe that an animal killed them, so you'll have to give me more than that," she said.

"I didn't say an animal." She raised her eyebrows at me. "But not human, either."

Jessica suddenly seemed more interested and moved forward to sit at the edge of the couch. "What are you implying?"

"I'm not comfortable sharing too much more at the moment," I said, wondering why the sudden change in her demeanor.

She gazed off, lost in thought for a moment.

"You said something about a dream or dreams, earlier. What did you mean by that?" I asked.

"That guy from the bar. I think he came to my house, but it may have been a dream."

I was out of my seat and on my knees before her. She looked shocked. "Tell me everything that happened," I demanded.

13

*J*essica

Liam was on his knees so fast, I hardly saw him move before he was demanding that I tell him about my dreams. This made me regret mentioning the dreams in the first place. Especially because the very dreams he wanted to know about all ended with him...and kissing.

How much should I share? Liam seemed to have information and so did I. Maybe some give and take was called for.

"What are you getting so excited about?" His expression was severe and his blue eyes were so intense, the color almost seemed to flicker.

"Just tell me everything you remember," he demanded. He seemed to realize how pushy he was being because he immediately softens his voice. "Please."

"Okay, but can you sit over there? I'm not certain if I want to kiss you or nail you with pepper spray," I said, only partially joking. He'd startled me when he reacted like that.

Liam smiled weakly, and color rose in his cheeks. Maybe, just maybe, he was surprised by his reaction as well. In some ways, it felt like I knew Liam, but in truth, I knew nothing about this man.

Liam slowly moved back into his chair but never took his gaze from me. His attention made me nervous for many reasons, not all bad.

Seriously, the man was like a ghost, with few public records. He could be anyone. Even serial killers could fake normal for a while. But I didn't get the creepy vibe from Liam at all. In fact, I suspected he acted cold or indifferent to hide a gentler nature. I'd seen too many glimpses of the man behind the mask to ignore it.

Although there was nothing gentle in his kiss. That was raw and feral, and it turned me on more than I cared to admit. I was drawn to Liam in a way that I'd never felt with another man. I couldn't put my finger on it, or explain it to myself, and explaining things was an essential part of my job.

"Well, to start with, that guy from the bar came to my house, but then the next thing I knew, he was gone, and I'd lost about an hour of time. It really shook me up. I was...*am* concerned that I may have had some sort of mental episode or maybe hallucinated the whole thing. Brain tumors can do that, you know. I interviewed a neurologist once," I said, feeling embarrassed admitting the situation to him, or anyone for that matter.

I was surprised to see his face go from anxious to angry as I spoke. I tipped my head to the side. "Am I upsetting you? I'm sure it's not really a brain tumor. Well, mostly sure. I tend to exaggerate things. It's an occupational hazard," I offered, trying to lighten the suddenly tense atmosphere.

"Jessica, I believe he did come to see you, which confirms my suspicions. The fact that your report aired tonight, and he showed up before that, tells me his interest is either personal, or he's trying to get to me through you," Liam said, his voice deep and rough with emotion. "Neither possibility is good for you."

"One, what would his personal interest be? And two, why would he think you would care about me?" I was trying to follow him, but none of this was making any sense. But then again, neither was finding a dead guy's fingerprints on a wine glass. Although I did have a theory about that, I just needed to speak with Zoey to flesh it out.

Liam looked wary, cautious even. As if the man from the first day we met had just shown up. I was even more convinced that Liam had secrets of his own. Were they from his past or something he was currently involved with? Did he have a secret wife? Or several secret wives? I had to rein in my wild imagination before it took me down a rabbit hole that led nowhere.

"I think he believes that you matter to me." Liam's gaze had me mesmerized. "I couldn't guess at his personal interest, but you're a beautiful woman, and you attract men like moths to a flame." His words both surprised me and made my insides flip. "I can't tell you how I know, but if you continue to report on this story, you could get hurt. And that would matter to me."

I fought the desire to kiss him again, and it was a real effort. It was like my body needed to touch him. Of course, his words had their effect on me as well. Even more so, since Liam didn't seem to be trying to seduce me any longer. He seemed sincere.

I made a calculated risk. "I stole his wine glass from the bar that night," I blurted before I chickened out.

Liam's eyebrows knitted together, then understanding entered his eyes. "And?"

"I had it dusted for prints in Phoenix," I added. His gaze stayed steady, but caution had crept into his expression.

"And what came back?" he asked. I wondered if he meant to say, *who* instead of *what*.

"Funny you should ask. The prints on the glass were mine, Zoey's, and a dead guy named Lorenzo. But not just any dead guy—one who died over twenty years ago. With mob ties, no less." I crossed my arms, watching to see if any of this seemed surprising or not. Liam didn't even blink, making me believe that he expected something like this.

When he said nothing, I added, "Oh, and his body was stolen from the morgue and never recovered. How's that for *creepy?*" I reached down, picked my wine glass up from the table, and tossed the last of the red liquid down my throat.

"Why don't you look surprised, Liam?" I asked, standing. Liam stood as well. He was at least six-foot-three, so I had to tip my head back to look at him.

"Because that same dead man was at the bar the other night. That same dead man came to your house. Have you discovered any wounds on your body?" he asked, deadpan.

"What?" I asked, my hand going to my chest. My heart started pounding like a scared rabbit, and the hairs on my skin stood on end. But not because of his odd question, but because in the back of my mind, it rang true and frightened me. I couldn't say the word *vampire* out loud yet, but I think one of us was going to before the night was over.

Liam had merely added validity to a notion that I had refused to entertain—until now. I'd stepped back from Liam when he asked the question. Not that I felt he was a threat, but because I wanted to physically distance myself from the reality he was beginning to present.

"The campers both had puncture wounds on their throats and no other injuries to account for their blood loss. Do you believe in *vampires*, Jessica?" I backed up further, and Liam followed me until I hit the kitchen table. So, he knew about the cause of death, too.

"You had to say it, didn't you?" I fumed. "More wine?" I asked, trying to change the subject.

"I just asked you if you believe in vampires, and you ask me if I want wine?" He was standing so close, and his nearness was messing with all my senses.

"I never discuss...*vampires* without alcohol." I slid to the right and away from him. I moved into the kitchen, pulled down my last two clean wine glasses because I wasn't going out there to retrieve the other two. I needed space to breathe and think. We were actually discussing vampires.

I poured two more glasses and picked them up to carry into the living room, almost running into my house guest in the process. Liam filled the small doorway into the kitchen with his broad shoulders and larger than life body.

Surprised, I almost dropped the glasses. To cover, I thrust his drink at him, causing some of the crimson liquid to splash out. It ran down the glass, onto my fingers, before landing on the floor. I ignored it.

He smiled at me and took the glass. "The answer is no. I don't believe in vampires, but the notion would make a fascinating documentary. There are actually people who believe themselves, vampires. It's a whole subculture sort of thing," I lied. The idea was becoming harder to deny, yet still seemed surreal and impossible.

I simply didn't want to entertain the idea. It meant a walk on the dark side, and I wasn't ready to go to crazy town just yet. He raised his eyebrows at me.

"Believing you're something doesn't make it real," I said.

"Not believing in something doesn't make it any less real," Liam challenged, then turned to the side so I could squeeze by him.

"Touché, Captain McKenzie." I was hypersensitive to my body brushing against his.

"So, for the sake of argument, let's assume that this

Lorenzo guy is a vampire, what would you do?" he asked. "The smart thing would be to leave it alone." I felt Liam's presence as he followed me into the small living room. It was like his aura was brushing against mine. If I believed in that sort of thing, which I didn't. Or, I didn't think I did. It went hand in hand with believing in vampires.

"I wouldn't be an excellent reporter if I ran away from tough stories," I said. I could tell he didn't like my answer by the way the muscles tightened in his neck. "What I'd really like to know is how Liam McKenzie fits into this story."

He became as still as a statue. A metaphoric clock was ticking loudly in my head, and I'm sure that I could hear a pin if it dropped.

Liam was tense again, and I was beginning to recognize the subtle nuances in his expressions. Soon, I'd be able to read those expressions faster than his verbal responses. I'd taken a class on reading body language, combined with facial expressions and what they meant. Liam's body language was wary and defensive.

"There's nothing to tell. I came across some information and wanted to warn you. This whole vampire thing is new to me. I'm no expert, but I do know there are things that exist, that defy explanation and maybe even science," he said.

I stared at him. "Well, as luck would have it, my boss is insisting that I retract some of the comments I made in my report, especially the one that suggests Flagstaff has a killer on the loose," I said, feeling angry. The community deserved to know the truth, despite the political fallout.

"I agree, but maybe the problem has already moved on," Liam offered, cryptically.

I kept my gaze steady as I looked at him.

"Those two people deserve to have their story told. They deserve justice. And personally, I think it's more likely that the dead guy never died. Somehow, he faked his death," I suggested.

Liam shook his head, and a flash of sadness crossed his features, but only long enough for me to wonder if I'd really seen it. "You leave me no choice," he said, standing. I watched, surprised, as he walked out the front door. I stared after him.

As I sat there wondering what just happened, he returned. Liam had a backpack over his shoulder, like something a college student would carry. I blinked at him in total confusion. I'm sure he could read it on my face.

"What are you doing?" I asked, a thread of panic seeping in.

"I'm staying the night. You won't accept the real danger that you're in, so I'll stick around and make certain nobody comes for you, dead or otherwise." There was a mixture of seriousness and humor in his expression.

I jumped up, when his intentions were clear. "You can't stay here!" I demanded.

"I'll sleep on the sofa," he offered.

"You don't fit, and...no!" I put my hands on my hips and set my chin—even though the thought of him spending the night made areas of my body burn with an invisible heat.

"Do you have a spare room, maybe?" he asked, looking toward the hallway, which was so small it could hardly be called a hallway.

"Yeah, the one filled with art. Liam, you can't stay with me. Do you know how insane this sounds? This is not happening, so just take your backpack and go." I tried to wave him to the door, but he didn't budge, and then we were way too close again. I crossed my arms over my chest and glared at him.

"That's okay. I have a sleeping bag and a pad in the truck. I'll sleep on the floor." He was not taking no for an answer, and it was infuriating and so darn sexy at the same time. I was one hot mess of a woman, conflicted on so many issues where he was concerned.

"Go get your sleeping bag," I said.

He smiled at me, and my heart wanted to melt, then he turned and walked out the door again. He'd left his backpack on the floor. Before I could change my mind, I took his pack and put it outside the front door. My heart constricted painfully as I closed and locked the door—locking Liam McKenzie out of my house, and maybe metaphorically out of my heart.

1 4

I woke to my new ringtone, *Happy* by Pharrell Williams. It was going to be my new mantra if it killed me. There was a happy place somewhere between career and personal life, but my job was in the tank, and I had no personal life to speak of. I'd just locked out the only man I'd been attracted to in over a year…and in truth, I'd never felt this way about any man before.

Picking up the cell phone, I turned it off and laid in bed while I went through the unfortunate events from the day before. I felt terrible about locking Liam out of the house, but there was no way I was letting some guy I barely knew invite himself to stay the night—no matter how sexy-sweet he acted. And no matter how much I wanted him to stay. Hell, my hormones wanted to have his babies.

Still, I felt so guilty when I turned the lock and flipped off the porch light. I went as far as darkening down the house so there'd be no doubt. I just couldn't let him stay the night, and he wouldn't take no for an answer. He'd left me no choice. If he ever spoke to me again, maybe I could explain myself.

I prepared for work in a rush. Had to look my best, in

case my career came to a screeching halt. If I was going down, I might as well go down with class.

Brenda was most likely gloating. I'm sure she'd heard about the ass-chewing I'd received. That sort of news made it around the station faster than election stats.

Today, I'd do the walk of shame, before writing my retraction and choking it out on camera. Let's see—a career in the toilet, any potential love-life also in the toilet, and either I have a brain tumor, or a dead guy really is stalking me. Doesn't get much better than this.

And what was I supposed to do about Liam McKenzie? I didn't even have time to think about that one. A dead guy stalking me might be easier to handle.

While I was lamenting on how much I was dreading this day, Daisy called.

I answered. "Hey, are you here already? I'm almost done. Give me a sec," I said, in a rush. It was hard to hold the phone to my ear, finish buttoning my blouse, and slip on my heels at the same time.

"Do you know there's a guy sleeping on your porch?" Daisy asked sarcastically.

No, no, no! Liam did not sleep on my porch last night—in this weather! It was freezing at night.

"You're kidding me," I said, running to the front window and peering sideways to see the porch.

"Nope. You officially have a squatter. Want me to call the cops?" Daisy asked.

Liam was stretched out on my porch on top of his sleeping bag, not even in it. He was laying on his back, fully dressed, with one arm thrown over his eyes. Why did his biceps have to look so nice?

"Jess, you there?" Daisy asked.

"Yes, I'm here, but don't call the police. It's just Liam," I said, releasing an exaggerated sigh.

"That's Liam?" Daisy said, sounding shocked.

"Yep. Give me a minute to talk to him, okay?"

"Why is Liam sleeping on your porch?" Daisy asked slowly.

"I locked him out last night, and he has this crazy idea that I'm in danger," I said, ending the call.

I poured a cup of coffee, picked up my briefcase, and took another deep, calming breath before I stepped onto the porch. I had to be careful not to step on Liam's sock-covered feet.

The noise from the door must have woken him, and he began to move a bit, still not removing his really big biceps from his face. The stubble on his jaw looked good, too.

Visions of him wearing nothing but a towel and that same morning stubble crept into my mind, and I squeezed my eyes shut to suppress the image. When I opened my eyes, Liam was staring lazily up at me.

"Is that for me?" he asked, pointing at the cup in my hand. I nodded and handed it to him. "You locked me out," he accused in the soft, gravelly voice of someone who'd just woken.

"I did. And I'm sorry, but—"

"But you don't trust me," he finished. I nodded. "I get it. You're smart not to trust people. You never know if someone is what they appear to be or not." Liam had moved to a sitting position on the porch. He took a sip of coffee and watched me with smoldering bedroom eyes that made me want to call in sick and stay home—with him. Why did he have to be so thoughtful and caring and…too darn sexy for words? *And after what I did.*

"I want to trust you, Liam. I do, but I also know you have secrets. And trust isn't built on secrets," I said. He didn't respond. "I'm really sorry for locking you out. Thank you for caring, but I'll be fine on my own."

I smiled weakly, then stepped carefully over him to get to Daisy's idling car. The air was cold enough that the exhaust made passing clouds form. Daisy was watching me as I climbed in, her mouth hanging open. I'd stolen a quick glance at the house to find Liam holding his coffee while his gaze bore into mine.

"You've got a lot of explaining to do. I think this calls for donuts," Daisy said, as she pulled away from the curb and drove down the street.

I tried not to look at Liam again, but somehow, I knew he was still watching as we drove away. I could feel his gaze like an invisible caress, and it made me imagine locking myself in a room with only him and ignoring the rest of the world forever.

And then I knew there was something wrong with my head. Either that or I was falling for Liam. None of these thoughts sounded rational. I'd never wanted anything like that with any other man. What was different about Liam?

WALKING into work that day was the hardest thing I'd done in a long time. Just as I knew they would, people continued to stare after greeting me with sympathetic gazes. Everyone but Brenda, that is. She was absolutely glowing with a fake smile plastered on her face. She made a beeline for me the moment I walked in.

I was so not in the mood for her.

I ignored her when she called my name by unpacking my bag, placing my laptop on the desk, and organizing some papers. "Oh, Jessica! I heard about what happened, and I want to tell you that even though it was way out of line, and incredibly erroneous, your report was fabulous," Brenda gushed. Her voice was like nails on a chalkboard.

I returned her fake smile with one of my own. "Why thank you, Brenda. You're so kind to say so. I'd love to chat, but I have a retraction to prepare for." Brenda lounged lazily against the wall of my cubicle, holding a cup of coffee. When she made no effort to leave, I added, "If you don't leave now, I'll dump that cup of coffee all over your passive aggressive face."

Brenda's eyes bulged, and her lips parted in a completely shocked expression. She finally found her voice. "You don't have to be such a bitch about it," Brenda huffed, as she turned on her heels and left.

I smiled. That had felt so good. If nothing else positive came out of that day, I'd be content with the memory of Brenda's expression. Nobody stood up to her rude comments and bossy nature. I was sure to hear about it later.

I worked on my retraction for most of the morning. The wastebasket was filled with my failed attempts. It was difficult to write what I didn't believe. Even harder to stand in front of a camera and say those empty words.

It was apparent that a killer was loose, and I explained that to Mr. Boss when he came down on me. He didn't care that I didn't have an official statement when I came to him with the story. Now that the crap was hitting the fan, I was a rogue reporter who ran with a story that wasn't sanctioned by the station. *Coward*.

Daisy carried the almost empty pink box of donuts into my cubicle and plopped down in the only other chair. "How's it going?" she asked, holding out the box to me. I took a jelly filled donut covered in messy white powder and bit into it.

Around a mouthful of donut, I replied, "Terrible. But I did just tell off Brenda."

"That's why she had that look on her face. I thought she ate something sour." Daisy laughed, then her smile fell. "I'm sorry. I know you're getting the short end of the stick on this one. Is there anything I can do to help, besides moral support and donuts?" Daisy said as she took a chocolate cake donut from the box.

"It is what it is. I knew the piece was risky, but it's news, and it needed to be shared," I said, slouching in my chair.

"You were given the green light. If Mr. Boss wasn't so spineless," Daisy said, lowering her voice. "Let's film the retraction, turn it in and go to the Burning Moon to drown your sorrows. The best Happy Hour in town." Daisy said with a hopeful look on her face.

I smiled weakly.

"There's nobody I'd rather drown with," I said.

Daisy brightened. "Okay, let's do this and be done with it."

"You're right. Let's get it over with," I said.

WITH A SINKING FEELING OF WRONGNESS, I filmed the retraction and apologized for making unsubstantiated assumptions about the deaths. It was all I could do to get it out, but we managed to get the film turned in for the nine o'clock news. My boss, the sheriff, the mayor, and Brenda Jeffery were happy. Everyone was happy except me.

I wanted to go home tonight and paint a dark, angry picture for therapy. After a couple of drinks, it would be good for a laugh the next day.

Daisy and I walked into the Burning Moon just before happy hour ended. A guy named Fred worked the bar, and we ordered doubles before the prices changed. "Is Zoey working tonight?" I asked the bartender.

"Yeah, she'll be in at eight," he said, moving down the busy bar to take the next order.

I spun around on my bar stool and surveyed the crowd, just in time to see Cole walk in. The youngest brother was looking handsome in the typical laid-back Flagstaff style. I remember wondering if they handed out a welcome package of jeans, hiking boots, and flannel shirts at the visitor's center. This time of year, even the women sported flannels.

Cole scanned the bar before noticing Daisy and me as we openly watched him. He seemed to blush but quickly gave us a big smile, before heading our way. "Looks like the McKenzie brothers are hard to avoid," I said under my breath. Butterflies began to flutter in my stomach thinking Liam may be meeting Cole here.

"Thank god!" Daisy said, openly looking Cole over from head to toe. Cole didn't seem to notice.

"Hello, ladies. Here for the happy hour?" he asked, taking the bar stool next to Daisy and angling it away from the bar so he could see us both.

"Maybe we're trying to pick up guys, and you're cramping our style," Daisy said, and I covered a laugh when Cole's eyes went wide before he realized she was teasing.

He smiled sheepishly. "I'll gladly sit in the corner over there if I'm bothering you," he said but made no move to leave.

"No need. We're just blowing off some steam. You missed happy hour prices, though," Daisy said, handing him one of her beers.

"Thanks," he said, and they clinked their bottles together and took a swig at the same time.

"Are Liam and Seth meeting you here?" I asked, not looking at him and trying my best to appear aloof. When he didn't answer, I looked over to find Cole and Daisy smirking at me, as if they knew what I was up to.

"No, he's at another bar," Cole said.

Hmmm. For the first time, I wondered if Liam had a girlfriend. There was no way that I was asking Cole that question. Daisy had said she thought all the brothers were single.

I did wonder why Liam was at another bar and Cole was here. They'd seemed close. Maybe they were but had different friend groups.

Just to defer any suggestion that I was interested in Liam, I asked about Seth. "Is Seth with him?" Daisy shot me a warning look like I was playing with her new toy or something.

"No, he's at the hotel bar across the street," Cole said, then looked like he'd said too much. Cole busied himself with tearing the label off his beer.

Daisy must have thought it was odd that they were all out at different bars as well because she gave me a strange look.

"Are they meeting up with you later?" I asked, not caring anymore if I sounded too interested or not. Cole seemed to be scanning the bar ever since he'd arrived. At first, I thought he was just nervous around Daisy and me. Now, I wondered what the brothers were up to.

I started to ask Cole when he stiffened. Cole's usually friendly demeanor turned fierce, and his head whipped towards the door. I followed his gaze and found Lorenzo Romano entering the bar. He spotted us immediately and smiled wickedly.

The tension in the air was palpable, starting with Cole's reaction, then mine, and then Daisy's. She had slid off her stool to stand close to Cole. I hadn't even shared with her that he may have come to my house, but she already knew about the fingerprints on the wine glass belonging to a dead guy. I guess that was enough for Daisy to freak out over.

Cole had his phone out and texted a quick message before Lorenzo reached us. I couldn't help but wonder; was this Lorenzo Romano? Did he somehow fake his own death? And if he did, who the hell was his plastic surgeon? He didn't look a day over thirty, but he'd have to be over fifty years old.

Whoever he was, he was walking right towards us, or me.

The way his bright blue eyes bored into mine made me want to run screaming from the bar.

Cole stepped in his way, and the two men glared at one another. Kudos for Cole. The other guy towered over him by a foot, at least, but Cole didn't seem intimidated. He just seemed angry as hell.

Ignoring Cole, the man turned his gaze to me, and suddenly, I wanted nothing more than to be with him. *Like he was the only thing in the entire world that I needed.*

*L*iam
        I arrived at the bar just after sunset. The first thing I did was order a beer, then sat in a corner where I could see the front door as well as the rest of the bar. Sipping my beer, I nodded at locals that I knew and settled into people-watching until the vampire showed up.

I'd only finished half my beer when my phone buzzed. It was a group text.

Cole: Vamps here

Tossing my beer back, I hurried out the door and drove a couple of miles to the Burning Moon. I knew Seth was just across the street and would arrive before me.

Seth was standing in front of the door to the Moon when I got out of my truck. He was peering into the window. "Is he still in there?" I asked.

"Yep. So is Jessica Parker," Seth said, turning away from the window to look at me.

"Shit." I pulled open the door and walked in. Seth followed.

The place was busy. I could see Cole and the vamp locked

in a staring contest, maybe on the verge of a fight. Jessica looked odd and didn't seem to notice me when I approached. Tonight, she only had eyes for *him*.

I came up behind the vampire just in time to hear Jessica say, "Let me go to him." That was when I noticed that Cole had ahold of one of Jessica's arms and Daisy had ahold of the other. Jessica stared longingly at the vampire, and I felt my blood begin to boil.

"What's going on?" I almost growled to anyone who wanted to answer.

The vampire slowly turned around to face me. White sparks flickered within the irises of his eyes.

"You again," said the vampire.

I wasn't sure what was happening to Jessica, but something was definitely wrong with her. She weakly pushed toward the vampire, but Cole and Daisy held her firmly. Both wore worried expression.

"You need to leave town. We know what you are and what you've done," I said, under my breath, so only he could hear.

The vampire smiled smugly. "And if I don't leave?"

I leaned close to his face. "I'll rip you to shreds."

He studied me, weighing the truth of my threat. "I wanted to take Jessica to dinner, what if I leave after that?"

I growled, and Seth put a hand on my shoulder. We were drawing attention that we didn't need. Seth was warning me to keep it cool in front of the humans. "Go near her again, and it'll be the last thing you ever do. If you want to live another day, you'll leave with us, now," I said, leaving no room for discussion.

From behind me, Seth said, "I do have the sheriff on speed dial. I'm sure he'd love to know where you were a few nights ago."

The vampire glared at Seth.

In a dull voice, Jessica said, "I need to go to him. Let me go with him."

Daisy looked frightened as she held her friend back. "Jess, what's wrong with you?" Jessica didn't respond.

"Daisy, take Jessica home and stay with her," I said, never looking away from the vampire. From my peripheral vision, I could see Daisy nodding. Cole helped Daisy guide Jessica around the tables and out the door. She seemed dazed and confused as she allowed them to lead her out of the bar with little resistance.

"A bit territorial, aren't you, Liam?" the vampire taunted.

I ignored the comment. "Let's go," I said, and stepped back to allow him to follow Seth out of the bar.

Cole was waiting for us out front. He nodded at me, and I took that to mean that Daisy had left with Jessica.

"You don't trust me to leave town on my own?" the vamp asked, seemingly amused.

"That's right. We'll drive you to the edge of town, and you can find your way from there," I said, as I motioned toward my truck. It was illegally parked in front of the bar. When we reached the curb, Seth opened the passenger door and motioned for the vampire to get in.

The man stopped and looked at each of us in turn, before sliding into the truck. I was on edge because I had no idea if he'd put up a fight or if the threat of being exposed would be enough to garner his cooperation. So far, he seemed compliant, which made me nervous.

I walked around to the driver's side, Seth slid next to the vampire, and Cole jumped into the back of the truck. We drove north toward Nevada in silence.

The vampire stared ahead, and I wondered what he was thinking. I would have been concerned about three shifters, myself. When we reached the edge of the county line, I pulled off the road and drove a short distance down an unmarked forest service road.

When the truck came to a stop, the vampire spoke. "You will regret this, you know."

"I regret that you ever showed up in our town," I said, getting out of the truck.

"Don't show your face again, or you'll regret it," Seth said, holding the door as the vampire exited the truck.

The vamp said nothing.

"Are we just going to let him go, after what he's done?" Cole asked.

For the first time, the vampire looked wary, as if he were prepared to bolt if need be.

"This time. There will be no second chance," I said, looking at the vampire. "Understand?"

The vampire bowed slightly. "Gentlemen. I hope you know this is not over. And there will be hell to pay—" The next second the vampire was moving faster than I could have imagined. He made it to the edge of the forest before he stopped and looked back at us, then disappeared.

"Well, that was creepy as hell. Do you think he's going to cause more trouble for us?" Cole asked.

"He's bluffing. Why would he have let us drive him all the way out here if he were going to do anything about it?" Seth asked.

"I think you're right, Seth. But I hope to never meet another vampire again," I mumbled, getting into the truck. Seth and Cole climbed in beside me, and I pulled the truck around and headed back to town.

"You should check on Jessica. She didn't seem herself. She kept wanting to go with that guy. I just followed Daisy's lead. She wasn't about to let Jessica go anywhere with him, even if she had to sit on her," Cole said.

"Yeah, what was that all about? Can vampires do that mind control thing?" Seth asked.

"That would suck," Cole added. "He didn't do it to me."

"Maybe he can't do it to shifters, only humans," Seth added.

"He did something to her. She told me that he came to her house, but she wasn't sure if it was a dream or real," I added.

"It kinda makes you wonder where Hollywood gets all their story ideas, doesn't it?" Cole asked.

"Maybe more people know about supernatural stuff than they let on. It would sure make me feel less alone, and maybe less of a freak," I said.

"No, you'll always be a freak," Seth teased, leaning forward to see me.

I smiled but kept my eyes on the dark road ahead. I thought about the campers who died by the vampire's hand. Maybe we should have handed down the only justice they'll ever see.

If Zoey is to be believed, a prison cell wouldn't have held him, so waiting for human justice was a joke. Did that make us the judge, jury, and executioner? And was I wrong to let him go?

I DROPPED Seth and Cole off in front of the Burning Moon. They were going in to see Zoey and have a celebratory beer. After all, we'd just chased a vampire out of Flagstaff, and maybe saved some lives. This thought went a long way toward relieving my concerns that we'd handled it all wrong.

Because I wanted to check on Jessica, I didn't join my brothers. Instead, I drove straight to her house. Daisy's car was still there, and the house was ablaze with light. I waited a few minutes then drove home.

I'd already concluded that I had no willpower to stay away from Jessica Parker. Confiding in Jessica would expose me, as well as Seth and Cole. If it went badly, we'd all have to disappear again and start over someplace new. Maybe she didn't have to know about me. But she'd made it clear that secrets wouldn't work. If I wanted a chance with Jessica, I'd have to come clean. I just didn't know if I could or should do that.

Either way, it wasn't a decision I could make alone.

When I pulled up to my partially finished cabin, I parked the truck but didn't go in right away. Instead, I sat there for a long time, thinking about the past and the future—all the limits I'd put in place to keep our secret safe. It was a lonely life. I was thankful for my brothers and the life we had carved out for ourselves, but I had to wonder if it would ever be anything more than what it was.

Finally, I stepped out of the truck and gazed up at the moon. Clouds floated around its glow. I peeled off my jacket and tossed it over the bed of the truck. I unbuttoned my shirt as I kicked off my boots, one by one.

The cold air stung my warm chest, but then it felt good, like a cold cloth to a fevered brow. I unbuttoned my jeans and pushed them down until I stood naked under the moon and stars. A blissful feeling of freedom washed over me and then I began to run until my wolf burst free, and then I kept running.

The forest was alive. I was hunting, tracking something or someone. I had their scent, and it was sweet and floral like springtime.

I came to an opening in the trees, and there she was. Not prey. My mate. A beautiful white wolf stood in the meadow bathed in moonlight, and she was all mine, only mine. She turned to look at me, and I somehow knew her name. The sound of it floating on air like a whisper. Jessica.

I'm overjoyed because she's my kind, but then a troubled thought creeps in, trying to steal my happiness. Is she like me because of something I did? Is she happy that we're the same?

I slow my approach, feeling uncertain. She sees my hesitation and comes to me. She rubs my neck with her muzzle. She radiates love and acceptance. We begin to run through the woods. Tonight, my queen is by my side.

Tonight, we hunt together.

I WOKE naked in my bed, the dream still fresh. I couldn't help but look around to confirm that I was indeed alone. Jessica was not with me and never would be.

16

*J*essica

I find myself in the forest at night. This should frighten me, but it doesn't. I'm home.

I see him running out from the trees. My great tan beast. His eyes glow amber in the light of the moon and his soft tan fur ruffles as he approaches. He's magnificent and powerful. He's my alpha. His name is a whisper on the air. Liam is what he's called. He sees me but hesitates. Why doesn't he come to me? I go to him, show him he's mine. I know the wolf from my dreams has come for me. And I want to run with him. And we do because we're free.

My alarm wakes me. Smiling, I stretch luxuriously, feeling more alive than I have in a long time. What a great dream. I'd been dreaming of wolves ever since I could remember but this time, I was the wolf, and it was incredible.

A noise directly next to me made me jump. A mumbling Daisy smacked her lips. She was laying on top of the covers, fully dressed. I looked down and realized that I was still wearing the clothes from yesterday. What the hell happened last night?

The last thing I recalled was seeing Cole, and...*Lorenzo?*

No matter how hard I concentrated, it was all blank after that. *Oh no! Did I black out again?*

I started shaking Daisy. "Daisy! Wake up. Wake up."

Daisy muttered something unintelligible and tried to roll away from me. "Daisy!" I yelled, and she sat straight up in bed, looking around like she didn't understand where she was. She blinked at me and relaxed back against the pillow.

"What time is it?" she asked, yawning.

"Six. Now tell me what happened last night. Did I pass out?"

Daisy must have recognized the concern in my voice. She sat up and looked at me with tired, worried eyes. "No, but you were acting really weird when that dead mafia guy showed up. Don't you remember?"

My shoulders slumped. "No, not a thing past Lorenzo walking into the bar." Daisy's eyebrows knitted together. "Please tell me everything," I begged.

"Well, he wanted you to go somewhere with him, and you were going to go. Cole and I held you back until Seth and Liam arrived—"

"Wait. Liam was there?" I asked, alarmed.

"Yeah, he told me to take you home and stay with you. He didn't look very happy. I thought he'd beat the crap out of that guy when he saw how you were acting. It was weird. You were like...in a trance. That's the only way I know to describe it. Cole and I had to physically restrain you from going with him." Daisy shook her head, and my mouth dropped open.

"You had to restrain me?" I asked, and Daisy nodded. "What happened after that?"

"I took you home, and the McKenzie boys were going to see Creepy Dude out of town. Seth threatened to call the sheriff if he didn't go quietly."

"Why didn't they call the sheriff? He's obviously involved with those deaths," I said.

"He's obviously a creature of the night, Jess. Haven't you been paying attention?" I rolled my eyes at her, but it was getting harder to deny. "His fingerprints match a dead Italian gangster whose body went missing. The missing body shows up in a bar, sipping wine and starting trouble shortly after two people are drained of blood. And we both know that the missing blood is how that guy doesn't look a day over twenty-something, even though he should be over fifty!"

"I guessed thirty-something," I grumbled. Daisy was getting really fired up. I could hear her fear through the sarcasm.

"Not a day over twenty-seven," Daisy scoffed, crossing her arms. She saw my smile. "This is serious, Jess." She looked annoyed and then looked away.

"I'm sorry. I know something strange is going on, but there has to be a logical explanation. We just need to figure it out before anyone else," I said.

"No, we need to get as far away from this whole situation as possible. I just hope Liam was able to convince him to stay away." Daisy threw her legs over the edge of the bed and stood up. "I'm making coffee. I can't think without coffee." I smiled as she left the room.

"I'll take a quick shower and join you," I yelled after her.

TWENTY MINUTES LATER, I joined Daisy at the kitchen table. She had English muffins, jelly, butter, and two steaming cups of coffee sitting on the table. Daisy was slicing an apple to add to the selection.

I sipped the coffee reverently, closing my eyes and sighing

long and slow. I noticed a bud vase on the table with a single white lily. It was beautiful, but it made me feel anxious.

"Where did that come from?" I asked, motioning toward the flower.

"That was lying on your porch when we got home," she said, wiggling her eyebrows at me. "Someone has a crush on you," she said in a sing-song voice.

I ignored her comment and stared at the rose. A feeling of dread filled me. "Do you know who left it?" I asked.

"I assume it was Liam. How many other admirers do you have?" she said, laughing.

I just stared at the rose. Daisy reached over and put her hand over mine. "Jess, what aren't you telling me? Who would it be from?"

"I don't know, but I don't think it's from Liam. That guy from last night came to my house after we first saw him. Before I knew about the fingerprints," I confessed.

Daisy's mouth hung open, and I felt guilty for not telling her sooner. She had become my closest friend and had supported me from the first day we'd met. Daisy should have been the first person I told.

"I'm sorry that I didn't tell you, Daisy. I was worried that I was having blackouts or something terrible like that," I said.

"Like some dead guy stalking you isn't terrible? Besides, even if you have something wrong with your head, which you do, obviously, you still should have told me." She looked hurt.

"Don't be like that. I wasn't sure that it even happened. One minute he was there and the next he was gone, and then I'd lost an hour of time," I said, realizing it sounded worse with each revelation. I really had been avoiding the truth.

"Jess, this is serious. You should call Liam and ask if he left the flower. I'd feel better if he had. I'd also like to know what happened after we left. I hope the guys are okay," she said, suddenly looking concerned for an entirely new reason.

"I don't have his number, only the station number," I confessed.

"Are you serious? The man slept on your porch, and you haven't exchanged numbers?" Daisy asked, incredulous.

"It's worse." I paused and bite my lip. "He kissed me again," I say sheepishly.

"Shut up, you did not!" Daisy says excitedly.

Daisy's eyes were as round as saucers, and she looked as though she might explode from excitement. Gone was her annoyance at my poor decisions or my lack of personal well-being.

"Tell me every detail. Was he a good kisser? I'll bet he was. How could that gorgeous specimen be a bad kisser? That would be like a cruel cosmic joke," she said, excitedly answering her own questions before I could. I laughed, relieved the subject and mood had taken a better turn.

When she finally settled down, I said, "He's either an excellent kisser, or it's just been so long that any kiss seems exceptional."

I knew Liam was a good kisser because I never wanted it to end. It was one of those kisses.

"I can't believe you held out on me," Daisy said, shaking her head. "I'm emotionally wounded, I hope you know." She pouted, making her point.

"I really am sorry. I meant to tell you. It's just the timing has been horrible, and I wasn't sure if something was starting with Liam and I didn't want to make a big deal out of it if it was nothing." I slumped in my chair and curled my fingers possessively around the coffee cup. "I'm still not certain."

Daisy tilted her head to the side. "What makes you think he wouldn't want a hot mess like you?" she teased.

"It's not that. There seems to be a mutual attraction, or at least I believe so. But Liam has secrets, and I don't feel confident starting something with someone who I'm not at least optimistic about trusting," I said.

"What could Liam have in his closet that would be that bad? Maybe he hasn't paid his taxes for several years. Or maybe he was arrested for drugs when he was a kid. Or, maybe—"

"Or maybe he's hiding something serious. He's convinced that the guy with the dead man's prints is a vampire," I said.

Daisy paused. "He said that?" she asked, incredulous.

"Well, he hinted at it, and then he asked if I believed in vampires."

"So, he brought it up? He didn't come right out and say *I think this guy is a vampire,* right?"

I rolled my eyes. "It wasn't that direct, but yes, he did—sort of," I offered.

Daisy scrunched her face up as if deep in thought. "Hmm. That is interesting. That explains his rush to get the guy out of town. Why or how would Liam know this?" she said, most likely thinking out loud.

She suddenly slammed her hands on the table, making me jump. My coffee sloshed out of the mug and onto my hand and dripping onto the table. "Really?" I exclaimed, grabbing napkins. Thankfully, it was no longer hot enough to burn.

"Sorry. What if Liam's a vampire?" she asked, her eyes going wide with the possibility.

"Nope. He's warm and hot-blooded. Too much so to be a vampire," I said, holding back a laugh.

"Then what about a vampire hunter? Hey! That could be it. I think we're on to something," she said excitedly.

"Do not include me in these delusions. I still expect to find a logical explanation for the fingerprints. I just need to talk to Zoey first."

My phone buzzed on the table, and I reached for it. My

boss's name showed on the screen. What was he calling so early for? I wasn't even due in today.

"Good morning, Ken," I said. Daisy pointed to an imaginary watch on her wrist and made a mad face that made me smile.

I listened for several moments as he spoke. Daisy watched me curiously.

"Yes, I understand. We'll get on it. Daisy's sitting right here. Okay. Thank you for saying so. I'll look for your text. Goodbye," I said, then ended the call.

"What was that all about? You look white as a sheet," Daisy said, looking concerned.

"There's been another murder," I said.

Daisy looked as shocked as I felt. "He's calling it a murder?" she asked.

"This time there's no doubt. He wants us to get to the crime scene ASAP. He'll text me the address."

"Well, crap. What a way to be vindicated," Daisy said sadly. "I'll grab my backpack from the car. Do I have time to take a quick shower?" she asked, on her way to the front door.

"Sure. Make it a quick one," I said, heading to my room to pull my wet hair into a slick bun. Mr. Boss had apologized for not backing me on the original report. I'd rather have been wrong about this. There was no positive spin on the price of proving me right.

"Jess?" I heard Daisy call from the door. I turned away from the hall and went to see what she needed.

Daisy was standing in the front doorway, looking back at me over her shoulder. This time, she was the pale one.

"What is it?" I asked, coming to peer around her. She stepped back, and I gasped.

My front porch was covered in dozens of long-stemmed white lilies. I remembered that white lilies were the flower for death.

17

$\mathcal{L}$iam

   I was still off shift for another couple of days. Cole and Seth were meeting me at the Toasted Squirrel for breakfast. We met there for breakfast or sometimes just a cup of coffee several times a week.

   There was more traffic parked along the streets than usual for this time of day. As I slowed the truck to a snail's pace, I saw police cruisers blocking the road and several groups of people milling about and talking excitedly about something. Their gazes focused on the street I needed to get to.

   One of the deputies that I recognized was redirecting traffic to turn around in the small empty parking lot of a bike shop. I stopped as I reached the deputy and rolled down my window. He recognized me and approached the truck with a grim look.

   "What's up?" I asked.

   "Bad news. I'm not supposed to talk about it," he said, looking around. "But I suppose you'd hear from the fire crew that responded." He still didn't look like he wanted to tell me,

133

so I stayed quiet and waited. Whatever had happened had him upset.

"It's Henry. He's dead—murdered, from what I hear," he said, shaking his head. "It's a damn shame. I don't know what's happening to our town these days."

The deputy didn't need to say more than Henry for anyone to know that it was Henry Yazzie, owner of the Toasted Squirrel Cafe. I dreaded the day I'd hear about Henry passing, but I always expected it to be from a heart attack or some other health-related issue, never murder.

"When did this happen?" I asked, feeling sick.

"It's still being investigated, but the best guess was after midnight and before three this morning," the deputy said, pushing away from the truck and motioning me forward.

I pulled forward with a heavy heart and too many troubled thoughts to count. I drove around the block to another street that allowed me to see the Squirrel from a distance. There were more police cruisers in the parking lot, and the restaurant was closed off with yellow crime scene tape.

My heart ached. I picked up my cell phone as it buzzed on the seat next to me. Seth was calling, and Cole had already texted me. "You see this?" I asked when I answered Seth's call.

"Yeah, I just pulled up. I see you. What's going on?" Seth asked. I spotted him on the opposite side of the intersection, sitting on his motorcycle, holding his phone.

"It's Henry. Someone murdered him last night, most likely after midnight," I said. There was silence as he must have been doing the math and trying to come to grips with the possibility that I still didn't want to face.

"Damn it all to hell!" he finally said. "Let's meet at the bakery on Aspen," Seth suggested.

"I'll let Cole know," I said, then ended the call. I sent Cole a quick text to meet us at the bakery.

When I walked into Sugar Bear's, there was a line at the counter. Seth and Cole were already sitting at one of the small metal tables. As I took a seat, a curvy woman with a pretty face set three cups of hot coffee down. "Let me know if you decide to indulge in a pastry," she said, smiling. Her name tag said, Helen.

"Thank you, Helen," Cole said, giving her a brief smile.

For a few moments, we just sat there. Maybe Cole and Seth were remembering Henry as I was. I finally broke the silence when darker thoughts intruded on the kinder memories.

"We need to find out how he died," I said, lowering my voice.

"What does it matter? We know why he's dead and who killed him," Seth said, his face turning red from anger and emotion. I remembered what our father said about Seth a year after our mother died. He said that Seth felt things more deeply than most but was good at hiding it or burying his feelings deep.

That entire year after our adopted mother had passed, I'd been jealous of the way Seth seemed to hold it together. I was the oldest, it should have been me handling the details and keeping things moving.

"We don't know that for sure," I said.

"Yeah, I think Seth's right, Liam," Cole said, looking as bad as I felt.

In my heart, I knew it was true. I just didn't want to admit that any of my actions contributed to the death of anyone, especially Henry Yazzie.

"All right, but we still need to be one hundred percent sure that the vamp killed our friend. Agreed?" I asked.

They both nodded. "If we confirm that Lorenzo killed Henry, we need to finish this, once and for all. Nobody else can suffer because I refused to take action," I said, keeping my voice low. Seth and Cole leaned closer so our conversation wouldn't be overheard at the busy bakery.

"This isn't all on you, Liam. We all made that call to force him to leave," Cole said.

"Cole's right. This was a mutual decision. We did what we thought was best," Seth offered.

"He killed those two campers, and I knew the police wouldn't be able to hold him, just like they couldn't hold Alistair," I said. "In the end, it's my call, and my responsibility."

Alistair Wilson was the shifter I killed over eight years ago. Knowing I didn't have a choice didn't make it feel any better.

Taking a life changed you in ways that were difficult to explain to others. It was a darkness that you kept locked down tight so that it never saw the light of day. It felt like a poison waiting to spread to every area of my life.

As if reading my thoughts, Cole said, "You don't have to carry another death alone. Let us help you do what we all know needs to be done. Damn it, Liam. We're family." I gave Cole a grim smile and patted his shoulder firmly.

We were family. We were a pack. We'd do what we needed to survive and protect those we cared for. This was our home. If we couldn't defend it, we didn't deserve to call it home.

I DROVE by the Toasted Squirrel one more time. There was still a lot of activity, and now the news vans were there. I spotted the KUTV van and a few from Phoenix.

From inside my truck, I scanned the area for Jessica. I was worried for her when I saw the way she reacted toward the vampire. And now that Henry had been killed, I was convinced that she would be the next target. Worse than that, I wasn't entirely certain Lorenzo's intentions were merely to kill Jessica.

I didn't know which would be worse, but I couldn't allow myself to think about that and keep my wolf in check. When I spotted her, I got out of the truck and headed toward her.

She was just finishing filming in front of the Squirrel. Daisy lowered her camera and gave Jess a thumbs up, but she wasn't smiling. I was standing on the opposite end of the yellow tape, surrounded by curious bystanders.

Jessica still picked me out of the crowd quickly. Her expression was one of concern and maybe relief. She motioned for me to join her. I skirted the taped off section of the parking lot and worked my way toward her direction.

Daisy nodded at me, then continued to review the footage she'd just taken. When I was close enough, Jessica surprised me by throwing her arms around me and giving me a brief hug.

I cautiously returned the embrace, taking in the scent of her. It was the same as in my dream. When she pulled away, looking embarrassed, I coughed to cover my own. "I…I was worried about you," she said, sounding uncomfortable with the confession.

The idea of her being worried about me, or even caring at all, made me smile. Then I remembered why we were there, and my smile faded, so did hers.

"Did you know Henry?" I asked.

"Didn't everyone?" she said, looking sad. "He was a great guy."

I nodded. "Do you know how he was killed?"

She and Daisy exchanged a look. "Same way the campers died is the unofficial word," Jessica said, looking over her shoulder at the restaurant. "You probably know that he lived alone in the house attached to the diner." I nodded again.

She looked like she wanted to say something. "What is it?" I asked.

Jessica looked anxious. "About last night…I don't know what I said or did. I didn't even know you were there."

Her words chilled me to the core. "I suspected something wasn't right. I'm just glad Cole and Daisy were with you. I don't want to think about what might have happened if he'd found you alone," I said, the anger coloring my tone

Jessica hugged herself. "I'm glad they were there too. There's something else." I waited for her to continue. "Someone left a white lily on my front porch last night." She bit her lip and looked up at me with a hopeful look.

I understood the question behind the statement. I shook my head, and her face fell. Seeing that look on her face was like a punch in the gut. "I'm sorry, but it wasn't from me. I wish it were," I added.

She smiled weakly at me then. "That's not all. This morning when I woke, the porch was littered with more white lilies."

My blood grew hot, and I had to turn away from her in order to control the rage boiling in me. My wolf was so close to the surface, if she looked hard, she might see it. I was shaking with anger. I needed to focus on my breathing.

A small hand touched my arm. I froze. Her touch had a soothing effect on my wolf. All I wanted to do was protect Jessica--needed to. But so far, I'd failed. What kind of alpha was I?

Finally, I turned around to find concern on her face. I wanted to hold her and tell her it would all be okay, but I didn't. I had no claim to her. Things were already confusing between us. I shouldn't push it further.

"Liam?" she asked.

"I'd take it as a threat, Jessica. You should not be alone." I pulled out a scrap of paper. "Do you have a pen?" I asked.

Daisy was there offering me a pen faster than I could get the words out.

"Thanks," I said, then wrote my cell phone number on an old receipt and handed it to her. "Call me, anytime. Don't hesitate."

She took the paper and held it. "Thank you, Liam."

That was enough proof for me. I knew who the murderer was, and I also knew he was sniffing around Jessica. I might have killed him for that reason alone.

"I'll be around town all day, if you need me," I said. I nodded at Daisy, who had been eavesdropping on every word. She waved enthusiastically.

I did reach up and touch Jessica's cheek, briefly. Then I turned and walked back to my truck knowing that I'd do whatever it took to keep her safe.

18

*J*essica

I stood there watching Liam's broad shoulders as he left. He was so beautiful. His concern was touching, and I could feel my resolve to keep my distance from him slipping each time I saw him. It was embarrassing not knowing what I said or did around a room full of people, but mostly because he was there. Daisy assured me that I didn't do anything too awful.

When Daisy and I returned from the murder scene, I noticed Brenda glaring in my direction. "Who rained on her parade?" I asked Daisy.

"Word has it that she threw a fit when Mr. Boss wouldn't let her take your story over," Daisy said smirking.

"Is that right?" I said, smiling warmly at Brenda until she huffed and ducked behind her cubical.

I was pretty sick about the death of Henry Yazzie. Partly because I'd been itching for a big story in this sleepy college town. But, I never wanted success at the price of three lives.

"Daisy, I'm stepping out to run an errand, but I'll be back before five. So, don't leave me stranded. The boss said I could use one of the company cars." I grabbed my jacket and started to leave.

"Where are you going?" Daisy asked, looking suspicious.

"I'm just running down a lead on a story. No big deal. I'll see you later," I said, hurrying down the hall before my self-prescribed babysitter decided to tag along. I loved Daisy, but I was used to doing things on my own. I was confident that I could go talk to Zoey in broad daylight without being attacked by a dead guy. If that indeed was what he was. Like the movies, he only showed up after the sunset.

I drove the company car, a black Honda Accord, to the bakery on Aspen Avenue and parked along the street. I'd pulled some strings and learned that Zoey lived in an apartment above the bakery which was only a couple blocks from the bar she worked at.

Looking up at the windows above the two-story bakery, I could see soft lacy curtains with dried flowers hanging from the same rod. The smell of baked goods permeated the air, and my stomach reminded me that I hadn't eaten lunch yet. I made a mental note to stop in at the bakery when I finished speaking to Zoey.

On the side of the building, there was an alley and a set of old wooden stairs that led to a landing and a single door. There were more windows on the alley side of the building as well, but only the second floor..

I went up the stairs and knocked on the door that was as dated as the stairs. I began to wonder when the last time a building inspector had been around. The curtains on the window moved aside a few inches, then fluttered shut again.

Seconds passed, and I started to wonder if I was being ignored. Suddenly, I heard the sound of a bolt being released and maybe a chain lock as well. The door opened, and Zoey greeted me with a cautious look in her eyes. I was used to it. Most people were wary when approached by the press.

"Hi, Zoey. I'm sorry to bother you, but I have a confession to make and a couple questions I'm hoping you could answer for me." I tried to give her my most disarming smile.

Zoey still looked at me as if I were dangerous but after leaning out the door to look both ways down the alley she invited me inside. She closed and locked the door behind us, which I thought was overly cautious, but maybe the old downtown area wasn't as safe as I'd always assumed.

Her small apartment was bright and airy, even though the actual footprint might have fit in a two-car garage in the suburbs of Phoenix. Zoey's apartment seemed to cover the entire front of the small building, and I wondered if there was another apartment behind hers.

I was dying to ask how much rent she paid, since I was paying through the nose for my tiny house, mostly because of its proximity to the college campus.

There was a strong scent of sage and other herbs in the apartment and I wondered if I'd interrupted her in the middle of cooking. She was wearing an apron over her jeans and t-shirt.

"Are you cooking?" I asked.

Zoey motioned for me to sit in an overstuffed pink chair. "Sort of. What can I do for you, Jessica?" she asked, getting right to the point.

"Oh, um—" I started.

"You said you had a confession and a question," Zoey prompted. She sat on one of the metal chairs next to the small two-person kitchen table.

"Yes. Well, my confession is that I stole a glass from the bar the other night," I said quickly. She said nothing, just watched me warily.

"You might be wondering why," I said, trying to encourage some back and forth conversation but still, she gave me nothing, so I continued. "I took the glass the Italian man had used."

There was a flicker of something in her bright green eyes, but it happened so quickly that I couldn't tell if it was a surprise, fear, or something else.

"Why would you do that?" Zoey asked.

I blushed. "Because I wanted to know who he was. We had two unexplained deaths in town, and a guy nobody seemed to know, starting trouble with the McKenzie brothers. I guess I did it on a hunch," I offered.

"And what would the glass tell you?"

"I had it dusted for prints," I said.

Zoey didn't try to hide her surprise this time. Her lips parted as if she wanted to say something but then thought better of it. "What did you find?"

"Well, that's what I wanted to ask you about." I toyed with the hem of my coat because the question I was asking was a long shot, but the only logical one I could come up with.

"What?" she said, and it came out as a whisper.

"Where did the wine glass come from?"

"The shelf, where all the wine glasses come from," she said, with a little annoyance.

"Is there a chance that it came from someplace else in the bar? Like could it have been taken out of storage…really old storage and used by mistake? Or maybe the owner purchased some glassware from an estate sale or something like that?" I asked, knowing that I was grasping at straws, but it was also my last refuge of ordinary.

"No." Zoey crossed her arms and cocked her head to the side to study me.

"Are you sure? Maybe someone else put an old glass up there and then you used it without knowing it was old," I suggested.

"No, I cleaned all the glasses that day. The glasses on the

shelf were the ones I personally cleaned and placed there," she assured me.

I felt myself deflate. "Well, that was the last straw," I said.

"Will you tell me what you found?" Zoey asked, leaning forward and resting her forearms on her knees.

"Would you believe the prints on the glass belonged to you, me, and a dead guy?" I asked, shrugging my shoulders.

Zoey stared at me for a long moment. I began to feel uncomfortable under her scrutiny.

"What did you learn about me?" she asked.

That was an odd question, since I'd just told her she served wine to a dead guy. "Only that your name was in the system. I wasn't interested in your prints. I knew your prints and mine were on the glass," I lied.

Zoey watched me closely, and I don't know if she believed me or not. "To answer your question, yes, I would believe you." Zoey leaned back.

I blinked at her. "Really?"

A bell sounded from what I believed was the kitchen, and Zoey stood. "I'll only be a moment. Want some tea or water?" she asked, as she headed into the kitchen.

"Some tea would be great, thanks." While she was busy, I let my eyes wander around the apartment. It was an eclectic style with Native American art mixed with antique glassware and strands of dried flowers and other plants hanging upside down throughout the cozy home.

If I had to sum up Zoey's space, I could do it with a few words. Old books, enough candles to open a shop, and dried flowers and herbs. Everything else seemed inconsequential in comparison. I wanted to know what she was cooking; the smell was strong and hung somewhere between inviting and maybe-not.

I picked up a book on the top of a stack piled on the floor next to me. It was leather bound, old, and smelled musty. I was almost afraid to open it, for fear of damaging the delicate pages within. Just as I was about to chance it, Zoey came out of the kitchen carrying two cups of hot tea. She noticed the book in my hand. My cheeks felt warm as I quickly replaced it, then took the mug she offered me.

"Thank you," I said.

Zoey didn't say anything about the book, but she didn't look happy about my snooping either.

"So, you would believe that the fingerprint of a guy who's been dead for twenty years just happened to be on a glass that only three people touched—you and I, being two of those people?" I asked, then raised the cup to my nose. It smelled of lemon and lavender.

"There are many things that can't be explained away so easily," Zoey said.

"Yeah, I've been hearing that a lot lately. But a dead guy walking into your bar and ordering a glass of wine doesn't seem unreasonable?" I asked, wondering if Zoey was a nut-job or just open-minded to weird possibilities. And what did that say about me? I'd gone as far as researching vampires and zombie voodoo. The information ranged from laughable to downright horrifying.

"Let me ask you a question, Jessica." I nodded, then took a sip of the tea, which was delicious. "Do you believe a dead man drank from that glass?"

There it was. This was the question that I'd struggled with since Lorie told me about the prints. Once I researched how improbable it would have been for Lorenzo to fake his death all those years ago, this was my last rational explanation. I thought that the gangster could have touched that glass years ago when it made its way into a box and only recently made its way back into circu-lation. It was a long shot but, in my mind, a real possibility.

"It seems impossible, but the facts are lining up that way. Do you know anything that might help explain it?" I asked.

"I do, but I think you already know. You just don't want to accept it, so you search for an explanation that is more to your liking," Zoey raised her eyebrows knowingly and sipped her tea.

"Why do you accept this...the supernatural explanation so easily?" I countered.

"That's my secret to keep. Not all secrets are bad, Jessica. Sometimes, we keep secrets for good reasons. Sometimes, secrets are kept to keep others safe. But most secrets are purely self-preservation."

She didn't mention Liam, but his name came to mind as if she'd said it out loud. Did she know his secret?

"Haven't you ever had a secret that doesn't affect anyone, except maybe you?" she asked.

I thought about it, but the only secret I held was my secret dream of being an artist. I guess it didn't hurt anyone but me. Being a news anchor was not my first choice and that was my secret.

I nodded.

"Did you know that art is considered in some cultures to be a form of magic," Zoey said, standing.

I blinked and sat up straight. Did I say that out loud?

Zoey smiled slyly.

"What made you say that?" I asked.

"I don't know. You give off an artsy vibe, I guess." Her smile, however, suggested a more profound knowledge. Now, I was looking for mysteries in everything. I had to be reading too much into her comment. I'd never told anyone but Daisy, and now Liam that I had any interest in art. Zoey couldn't know about my love of art. Could she?

I thanked her for her time and the tea. As she showed me to the door, I stepped out of the apartment and turned around. "I have to ask, what are you cooking? It smells… interesting." That was the most polite word I could come up with, short of lying, and I didn't want to do that with Zoey Espinoza. I had the distinct feeling that she'd know.

"It's an old family recipe. I don't think you'd like it much," she said, winking. "When you're ready to deal with the truth, come see me. I may be able to help." She smiled and closed the door before I could reply.

19

*L*iam

Homecoming weekend meant people started celebrating on Wednesday and didn't stop until Monday. It would make sense that the vampire would want to take advantage of the crowds. I felt the odds were good that we might spot him.

Cole, Seth, and I agreed to divide up and roam from one party spot to the next until we found the vampire. This time Seth was at the Moon, I was at the Weatherford hotel, and Cole was working the streets by following the college crowd from one house party to the next. He'd hit some bars if he had time.

That was the only way to protect Jessica and the community. I wasn't looking forward to killing anyone again, even a vampire, but I'd do what I needed to do. I didn't like this idea of vigilante justice, but what choice did we have?

We'd been at it all night with no sign of our target. I was tempted to call it off for the evening, but my sense of urgency prompted me to stick it out a while longer. It was all I could do not to stake out Jessica's house, but if we didn't catch this guy, she'd be walking around with a target on her back, and impossible for me to protect her.

It was a good thing that I stayed. Just before midnight, a couple walked into the hotel bar. Having been exposed to the scent, I knew right away what they were. Seeing two more vampires in town made the hair on the back of my neck stand on end, and my wolf stirred restlessly.

The vampires must have been able to sense my kind in some way because they picked me out of the crowded bar immediately. The man and woman made their way to a table on the opposite end of the room.

They continued to steal cautious glances at me. The woman's thin face was striking under a head of long white-gray hair. She didn't look older than early thirties. Her high dark brows were a dramatic contrast. The she-vamp's willowy figure moved with liquid grace, like a cat.

The male was notable in that he too made an impression. His dark brown, shoulder-length hair was pulled back in a ponytail, his features suggesting an Anglo-Saxon European heritage. He was equally as exotic as the woman.

The waitress went over and tried to offer them menus, but they refused them. She walked away, then returned with two glasses of red wine. The woman took a small object from within a beaded handbag that she'd placed on the table.

Curious, I watched as she opened the top and tapped a few drops of red liquid into the wine glass before returning it to her handbag. She noticed me watching and raised her glass toward me, then took a drink.

It only took seconds before I caught the scent of blood. I inhaled deeply, then raised my beer to her. Her face was difficult to read, so I wasn't sure if her message was taunting or friendly. I only needed to know what her kind did to three innocent people to know I didn't want them in my town.

Under these circumstances, they were guilty until proven innocent, and my money was on guilty.

I picked up my cell phone and sent Seth and Cole a warning about the two new vampires. My phone began to blow up with messages from both my brothers.

Seth: got two vamps here at the moon
what do we do now

Another message from Cole chilled me to the bone.

just found three
hanging around outside a college party
two men and one woman
WTF!?

I glanced up from the phone to see the vamps were gone.

Liam: meet at the moon
these vamps left
any eyes on Lorenzo

They both replied with *no*. That meant we had eight or more vampires on the loose in Flagstaff. It was like a damn vampire convention. Had Lorenzo called in reinforcements because he was seeking revenge on us?

I settled my bill and hurried down the street to the Moon. The streets and bars were crowded and would be for several more days. I spotted Seth but pulled up short. He was talking to two people, an attractive young brunette, and a well-built black man. Both could pass for college students—*if they weren't vampires.*

I came to stand next to Seth and eyed the other two. Neither looked like they cared what we were, and they certainly didn't seem threatened by us. "Liam. This is Olivia and Simon. They're...new in town," Seth said, looking around to see if anyone was listening.

Neither Simon or Olivia offered their hands, which was just as well. I wasn't feeling friendly. "What's the story?" I asked Seth.

"Olivia says her family just moved to town last week," Seth said, raising his eyebrows. I got what he was saying.

Olivia had long brown hair, cut in soft layers. She was small and petite, like Zoey, but she radiated strength in her tiny frame. Her eyes were smudged with the dark shadow that made her light amber eyes more dramatic than they already were.

"Is that right? And how long will your family be visiting?" I asked, playing along for anyone who was listening.

"We've relocated here. The head of the household likes the fresh air and the smell of pine trees," Olivia said sarcastically.

For all of her bravado, I couldn't help but notice that her eyes kept landing on Seth, and he seemed attentive to her every word. What the hell was going on here? Simon held silent, seemingly comfortable allowing Olivia to do the talking. His eyes were green, but just as light and somewhat iridescent as Olivia's amber ones.

Cole walked up, pulling up short, as I had. "What the hell? Are we just one big happy fricken family now?" He sounded disgusted as he glared at the vampires.

"That's right. We're going to start howling at the moon and dancing naked around a bonfire soon. Want to be the virgin sacrifice? It could be fun," she mocked. She winked at Cole and took a sip of beer.

Seth started chuckling, but Cole looked like he was about to lose it. I placed a hand on his shoulder to reassure him. "Easy, Cole," I said, close to his ear.

He was breathing hard, and I could sense his wolf was close to the surface.

"Down, boy," Olivia teased. Cole started to lunge at her, but Seth and I held him in place. Olivia laughed. Simon had also moved, placing himself between Olivia and us.

Seth gave her a disapproving look over his shoulder.

Surprisingly, she cast her eyes down as if maybe she felt bad for teasing Cole.

When Cole had himself under control, Simon moved back to his casual posture next to Olivia but kept his gaze on Cole. It wasn't clear what their relationship was. He was undoubtedly protective of her. That much was clear as crystal.

"Now that we've all settled down, the guy we're looking for is part of Olivia and Simon's...*family,* but Olivia here isn't too fond of him, if you know what I mean," Seth said, grinning at Olivia. She didn't smile back—*thank all that is holy.*

Could Seth be flirting with a vampire? I'd always known he handed out the charm indiscriminately, but this took it to a whole new level.

"Why would you help us?" Cole demanded, still not liking our present company.

"Maybe I'm not helping you." She finished the last of her beer. "Maybe I'm hurting him." With that, she glanced at Simon. He nodded and followed closely behind her as she brushed roughly past us and out of the bar. We stared after them until they left.

"Damn, I think I'm in love," Seth said, staring after her. Cole and I looked at him like he'd just lost his mind. And, apparently, he had.

"Are you crazy? Did you not get that she's a vampire?" Cole said, heatedly. "What about Henry?"

Seth dropped the silly grin and turned to Cole. "She said that was Lorenzo, and that he would be punished for it," Seth said. "She said they are out looking for him tonight."

"And you believe her?" I asked, surprised.

"I do. Something in her words rang true. She didn't have a beef with me, but she does seem to hate that Lorenzo guy," Seth defended. "Olivia said that Lorenzo's actions put them all in danger."

"Then you're dumber than you look," Cole said harshly.

"Watch it, little brother," Seth warned, all playfulness gone.

The last thing I needed was fighting amongst ourselves. I stepped in between them.

"That's enough. We have bigger problems. I don't need the two of you at each other's throats," I said. "Same team, same pack, same family, remember?"

Cole seemed to relax slowly, and so did Seth. I knew we were all strung tight and thin from losing Henry. And maybe, like me, they blamed themselves. His death hit us all hard.

"I have to be honest with you, Seth. I don't know if I buy her story. It could be a trick. Watch yourself, all right? She's not like other women, and we are at a huge disadvantage by not knowing anything about them," I said.

He nodded and reached his hand out to Cole. Cole hesitated for only a second, then grasped Seth's hand and pulled him in for a hug.

"Did she say how many were in her family?" I asked, Seth.

"Yeah, she said there's eight total, including Lorenzo. She called it a coven. I asked her what a coven was, and she said it was like a family but not," Seth said.

"Eight vampires? What are we going to do? We can't handle eight. We don't even know if we can handle one," Cole complained.

"Either we figure it out, or we leave," I said, and they grew quiet.

"I'm going to check on Jessica. I don't like that we saw so many vampires and not one of them was Lorenzo," I said.

"You falling for Jessica, big brother?" Seth said, sounding truly curious.

I looked between the two of them, both waiting for my reply. "It's something. It's like I can't get her out of my head. I'm even dreaming about her," I confessed. This was not a

R.K. CLOSE

comfortable conversation to have, even with the two people I was closest to. "There may be something to that fated mate idea, Seth. I'm just not certain how to handle it," I said.

Cole clasped my shoulder and squeezed. "It had to happen eventually. How's she feel about you?" he asked. I laughed.

"What does it matter? It's not like I can do anything about it," I said, shrugging his hand off.

"What's that supposed to mean?" Seth asked, crossing his arms over his chest.

"How can any of us have an intimate relationship with the secrets we keep? That's not the sort of skeleton you can let out of the closet." I ran my hands through my hair, thinking again that I needed a haircut. "Hi, I'm Liam. I turn into a wolf. Want to go to dinner?" I said, sarcastically.

"A big bad-ass alpha wolf," Seth corrected.

We shared a laugh, but it was gone quickly.

"I never gave it that much thought, but I think if you meet someone special enough to marry, we'd tell them, right?" Cole offered.

"That's my take, anyway," Seth agreed.

"We can't risk that every time we like someone," I said, looking at them like they spoke a strange language.

"Yeah, only when you think it's the right woman," Seth said. "Did you really think we have to be alone for the rest of our lives?"

I thought about this for a moment. It just didn't add up. Or maybe I didn't know I could trust another person with a secret that could potentially impact all three of us. I didn't answer him.

"Well, I haven't met the right woman yet, but I think there must be one who can handle my wit and charm," Seth said, smoothing his hair back in a James Dean impression.

"Same. I don't want to be stuck with only you two clowns

for the rest of my life. I mean, you're cute and all, but..." joked Cole.

"I didn't know that you felt this way. I've been so focused on keeping a low profile—" I said.

"We know. It's been obvious the way you only date women who are passing through town or on vacation. Did you think you were sneaky about it?" Seth said, laughing.

I huffed. "I guess not," I said, shaking my head. "I didn't really know that's what I was doing," I said. But Seth was right, I realized. How had he been so observant about me, but I'd been clueless?

"Go check on your girl," Cole urged.

"She's not my girl. And don't forget she's a reporter. Wouldn't we make a great story?" I asked, in a warning tone. This was the main reason I'd tried to stay away from Jessica Parker. Maybe if I had, she wouldn't be in danger.

20

a pain in my neck woke me just as the sun was rising. My muscles ached from sitting in the same position too long. When I left Seth and Cole the night before, I drove over to Jessica's to make sure she was safe.

Daisy's car was in the driveway, so I figured she was staying close to Jessica as well. I was glad that Jessica had a friend like that. My plan was to leave before she knew that I was there, but as with the best of intentions, that didn't happen.

Jessica, holding a cup of coffee, was watching me from her living room window. I started the engine and let it idle for a minute while I watched her. We didn't wave or acknowledge each other, but somehow I felt close to her. I knew that thought was crazy.

Pulling my eyes from hers, I slowly pulled away from the curb and drove home for a shower and some real sleep. Hopefully, she didn't decide to file a restraining order on me.

I DREAMED of Jessica and the forest again. But this time we were merely us, running through the woods. It was playful and secretive. Then the day suddenly turned to night, and I couldn't find her.

I searched and called her name in vain for what seemed like a long time, and then I saw a light. Following the glow, I came to a clearing that I recognized. A tall bonfire blazed, and there were people standing around its flames.

I was back on the farm where I grew up. The same field where I dreamed about killing Alistair Wilson, the pack leader. But Alistair wasn't here now, and neither were his pack. These were vampires— eight in all.

The four females and four males stood, watching me approach. Movement caught my eye and I saw Jessica as she moved from behind Lorenzo. She said my name, but he grabbed her and held her close. I could feel my wolf coming alive. It wanted to tear into Lorenzo until he was no more than pieces.

He laughed, and I could see his white fangs flash like diamonds reflecting the fire. I began to run, but it was as if with each step I took, they grew further away. Jessica's frightened face tore at my heart as I tried in vain to reach her.

And then, keeping his eyes on me, Lorenzo bit into the soft, creamy flesh of her neck. Bright red blood began to run down her chest from his mouth. I roared my fury.

I WOKE to a dark gray sky that matched my mood. The dream would haunt me for a long time to come. It felt all too familiar. It was after four in the afternoon. I slept the day away. I made myself a cup of strong coffee and went outside to sit in a folding chair to drink it.

The same feelings of helplessness I'd felt eight years ago were returning. I was at a turning point. The situation with the vampires moving into our town meant trouble that could result in exposing us for what we were and worse.

There were many reasons to leave. We could protect our pack, keep our secret safe—survival.

Then the reasons to stay began with Jessica and ended with the community we'd become a part of. In many ways, they were like our family. From Zoey, Daisy, and Fred, the auto mechanic who let Seth live above his garage and use his equipment, to Henry, who had always had a table ready and a smile.

Then there was Bell, who owned a bakery, and regularly sent an extra box of pastries to the station with Cole. The list went on and on. I'd taken all our friends for granted until now when I considered leaving them behind. Who would protect them if we left?

And if we couldn't make it work here, would we ever find a home?

———

COLE, Seth and I were still off shift for another day. I'd made a decision about one issue in my life but didn't know if anything would come of it. I planned to talk to Jessica and see where we stood. Maybe she wasn't interested in dating a blue-colored firefighter. She had some lofty goals from what she'd mentioned. Seth always accused me of overthinking. Perhaps that was what I was doing now.

Would dating Jessica mean that I had to confess every-thing? I didn't know, but she'd made it clear she didn't care for secrets, and she was intuitive enough to have figured out that I had some.

I stopped by Seth's apartment so he could change my spark plugs while I waited. It wasn't like I couldn't do them myself, but he had unlimited use of all the equipment at

Fred's Auto Shop, making it a no-brainer. Besides, Seth loved to tinker with anything with an engine. It was a hobby for him. This was my contribution to his personal happiness.

The sun had set, and I was anxious to make sure Jessica was safe, and possibly start that conversation with her. That is if I could get her away from Daisy. That woman was better than a guard dog. I hadn't been arrested as a stalker, which was a good sign.

My phone buzzed, and I fished it out of my pocket. A second later Seth's phone began to sound as well. He wiped his hands on a greasy towel and picked it up.

I looked at Seth at the same moment he glanced up at me. We'd received the same fire alert. Last year the department had added a program where off-duty firefighters could respond to large-scale emergencies if they chose. This was the first real alert we'd had since the program was implemented.

Details about the emergency were included with the text message. We were to text a number one to respond, or number two to decline with no explanation necessary.

I nodded to Seth, and we both hit one to respond. A large-scale fire had broken out in one of the oldest dorms on the college campus. The buildings had been retrofitted to meet most of the newer building code requirements for fire safety, but not every detail of the current codes could be satisfied with the older architectures.

This fire must have been severe for extra firefighters to be called in. Seth closed the hood of my truck and got in. "I'd just finished anyway. Let's roll."

We could see the flames from Wilson Hall as we drove down the main drag in town, on our way to the fire station to grab our gear. Cole pulled up in his Jeep just as we arrived. It took us less than a minute to put on our turnouts and find some extra Self-Contained Breathing Apparatus or SCBA, as it was referred to. Once we had our fire turnouts on, we loaded the extra SCBAs into the bed of my truck and headed for the campus.

Since this was Homecoming week, the campus was even more packed than usual with families, and graduates returning to the small town and filling up all the lodging. I honked the horn to get bystanders to move out of the way so we could get as close as possible.

When they realized we were firefighters, they moved over to let us get past. A sheriff's deputy started to stop us, but when he approached the truck and saw who we were, he motioned for us to pass. I parked fifty yards from the engine, and we piled out of the truck.

I found the captain in charge and let him know we were on scene.

"We've got three students who aren't accounted for. One lives upstairs on the west wing, and the other two have dorms on the lower level. Until we know differently, they're all believed to be in Wilson Hall when the fire broke out," Captain Murphy yelled over the noise.

"Why isn't the fire contained?" I asked.

He shook his head. "Sprinkler system was turned off, and the nearest hydrant was vandalized to the point we can't access it. We've had to pull lines from other hydrants that aren't as convenient," he said.

Arson. I looked at Wilson Hall, the roof almost completely engulfed in flames, and wondered if anyone could possibly survive that.

"Where do you want us, Captain?" I asked.

"You three pull a line and do a sweep of the lower level to find those students," Captain Murphy ordered.

I turned to Cole and Seth. "Seth, you and Cole, start a line. We'll enter around back," I said.

After Seth and Cole had pulled a water line, we met at the

back of the dorm. We reached a rear entrance that looked like a maintenance entrance, but it was locked. I felt the door for heat. Finding it cool to the touch, I stepped back and nodded to Seth. He stepped forward, and with one mighty kick, the door crashed inward. Thick dark black smoke spilled from the doorway..

Visibility was impossible. Seth led with the hose. I put my hand on Seth's shoulder and Cole did the same on my shoulder. We stayed together this way, slowly moving around objects and basically feeling our way into the building by touch alone. Since we were working blind, the hose line was our way out when the time came. Our turnouts and SCBA tanks and masks kept us from inhaling smoke.

So far we'd not encountered any flames, just smoke. If there had been flames where we'd been, our turnouts would have protected us from the intense heat.

We were familiar with most of the dorms and buildings on campus, which helped me determine when we'd reached the residents' hallway for the lower level.

By luck or fate, we found a person unmoving and unresponsive inside the first room. I ordered Seth and Cole to follow the hose line and get the victim out of the building while I searched for the other. It was against protocol for me to work alone, but I had some advantages that ordinary humans didn't.

The dorm room was small, and it didn't take long to search. I moved slowly down the hall to the next room. I began the search by working my way around the edges of the room and furniture with one hand and reaching out and away with the other.

My outstretched hand connected with something, and I stopped to investigate. It was another victim. With some effort, I managed to grab ahold of them under the arms and began to pull the person out by memory and occasionally having to stop and feel my way before dragging them along. I no longer had the hose line to follow, which slowed my progress even more.

The timbers groaned loudly just before a portion of the upper level gave way and crashed down in front of me. I covered the victim's head as best as I could to prevent debris from injuring them--if they were even alive. There was no way of knowing until we made it out.

A large piece of debris now blocked our original exit route. I pulled the victim into another dorm room that I hoped was not destroyed by the collapse. Once inside, I left the victim for a moment to assess the wall that would get us past the collapsed floor and closer to the exit.

I said a quick prayer of thanks when I realized the wall was made of plasterboard and lumber. I could bust my way through that, but brick would have taken me too long. Without the advantage of my enhanced strength, we wouldn't have a chance.

It was circumstances such as this where firefighters lost their lives while trying to save others. That was not happening tonight. I began to punch the wall again and again until boards splintered, and drywall exploded. Once there was a hole big enough, I pulled the victim over to the opening, stepped through, then reached in and pulled them after me.

I thought I saw some light through the smoke and moved toward it. Two firefighters, who turned out to be Seth and Cole, helped me pull the victim out of the building while I collapsed on the grass to catch my breath.

Dragging a body through a building where you're working blind and wearing over forty-five extra pounds of gear is strenuous work, even for a shifter..

Paramedics placed the victim on a gurney and hustled them away. Seth and Cole found their way back to me and helped me up from the grass. I pulled off my SCBA, they had already removed theirs.

"What about the third one?" I asked breathlessly.

"They showed up. They'd been out drinking when they heard about the fire," Cole said. We walked back to the staging area to get some water and rest a bit. The fire was still being worked, but they were getting it under control.

Someone handed me a water bottle, and I chugged it. I pulled off my gloves and wiped the sweat from my forehead that kept running into my eyes. That's when I spotted the KUTV news van. A quick scan of the scene and I located Jessica and Daisy getting ready to report. Maybe I'd get a moment to talk to her, after all.

Then I remembered how dirty and sweaty I was and thought better of it. We still had work to do here.

The captain walked up and looked us over. "I want all three of you checked out by the medics at the rehab tent," he ordered.

"We're fine, just catching our breath," I said, trying to decline.

"This is not a request, Captain McKenzie. You boys know the drill. Besides, this is the first time we've implemented this backup program. I'll have hell to pay if they read my report and learn I didn't follow protocol," the captain said, ignoring my resistance. "Don't worry, we've got this wrapped up. You did good work." He nodded toward the rehab tent and then walked away.

21

Jessica

A fire was news. A massive blaze in one of the original and oldest dorms on the college campus was big news. Having just overheard a conversation between a couple of paramedics, discussing how the fire was suspected to be arson, made this the Flagstaff story of the year. Excluding the possibility that a vampire may be killing tourists and locals, that is.

If I presented a story on the vampire theory, I'd be laughed out of a career. I was beginning to wonder if that would be such a bad thing.

Daisy and I had just arrived on campus and were busy setting up the shoot. I was preparing to go live before Brenda Jeffrey could steal yet another story. The tables had turned when I snagged the story about the murders before she did. I planned to keep that momentum going.

Daisy had the lights on me, so I had to pretend I wasn't totally blind. More than once I'd tripped over cords and other objects after she would cut the lights.

"Hold up. Something's wrong with the camera. I think it's a loose cable. I've got another one in the van," Daisy said.

I put my hand up to shield my eyes, but she was just a shadow as she disappeared around the back of the van. The campus was packed with people, and the police were busy keeping bystanders at a safe distance from the active fire and out of the way of the firefighters.

I wondered if I'd see Liam and his brothers. I'd planned to look for him after we filmed this clip, but I didn't think they were working tonight. Still blinded by the lights, I turned to watch the fire behind me, while I waited for Daisy to return.

I turned around, only to come face to face with Lorenzo Romano. He was standing so close to me I had to look up to see his face. His smile froze me in place. Lorenzo glanced down, and I followed his gaze—just in time to see him unplug the extension cord for our lights.

It went dark for a moment. I was blinded again. Faster than I could think, he grabbed me and covered my mouth with his hand.

I heard Daisy from a distance. "Hey, who cut the lights?"

THERE'S that moment between sleeping and waking where you're partially aware of the dream you're leaving and the world you're waking to. It's like having a foot in two different realms, both trying to pull you further into one or the other.

I could smell smoke first. It made me wonder if I were still on campus. But I couldn't hear the nearby traffic, the shouts, and commands of the first responders, emergency sirens, or people crying and speaking in excited voices.

There was the sound of popping or cracking. My mind recognized this as a fire burning. I finally opened my eyes, and a great bear stared at me. I sat up quickly but realized that it was only the stuffed head of a bear hanging on a wall.

I was alone in a small rustic cabin. The many stuffed animal heads on the wall and the sparse furnishings told me that it was a hunting cabin. The floors were bare wood, except for a couple of simple rugs.

There were three doors and five windows. Three of the windows had Indian blankets nailed above as curtains. The other two had shabby beige curtains. Some were partially held back by a small clamp. The sky was dark beyond the windows.

One of the doors may have been for a bathroom. I could tell the others led outside.

I had no memory of how I arrived and no idea of how long I'd been here, but I did remember seeing Lorenzo. Panic was setting in, but I forced it down with everything I had. It was critical that I keep it together.

My brain kept screaming the same thing over and over —*Lorenzo is a vampire, Lorenzo is a vampire.* I concentrated on controlling my breathing. Was Lorenzo still here? I climbed off the cot I'd been lying on and cautiously moved to one of the windows. The moon was still bright enough to cast a little light. I could only make out the vast forest, but little more.

I moved to each window and peered outside. There were no vehicles, so maybe he had left. The dark forest frightened me, but not as much as staying in that cabin until Lorenzo returned. The vampire scenario had taken hold in my mind, and I couldn't shake it. As impossible as it seemed, I believed it was true.

Even if Lorenzo had been just a man, I would still be in serious trouble. Did Daisy know I'd been taken? Was she all right? I know there was a lot happening at the scene of the fire, but how did he manage to bring me here without anyone knowing?

A terrifying thought occurred to me. The night he came to my home, I lost an hour of time. Daisy told me the night at the bar, I wanted to leave with him, even though I have no memory of any of it. What if I left with him willingly? Nobody would have questioned him. I knew that Daisy would never have allowed me to leave with him. I hoped she was safe.

I rummaged through the drawers next to a small sink. There were flatware and a few cooking utensils. I finally located what I'd hoped to find—a long carving knife.

Carefully, I turned the handle to the door that I assumed was the back of the cabin. It was cold, even with the fire in the fireplace, but beads of perspiration began to run down my face despite the temperature.

The doorknob made too much noise but turned easily. I slowly pulled it open and peered into the trees beyond. It seemed nothing moved, and even the animals and insects were silent. In my gut, I knew that wasn't normal.

I couldn't stay and wait for him to return, I would rather face the dangers in the woods and even the risk of being lost in the forest, than face a dead man and whatever nefarious intentions he had.

My heart was pounding loudly in my ears, and I was beginning to feel faint. I realized that I was on the verge of hyperventilating and squeezed my eyes shut until I forced my breathing to slow. I could not afford to pass out.

I sprinted across the open area that surrounded the cabin and into the forests. I'd barely passed the first row of trees when I tripped on something and fell hard.

The memory of my mother warning me not to run with a sharp object in my hands, came to mind as my hand holding the knife scraped across the ground.

I pushed up from the ground and ran again, but this time

I moved more cautiously, trying to avoid the shadowy obstacles that might trip me up again.

The moon shone through the trees, and I wished I knew what direction I was heading. My primary goal was to put as much distance between me and the cabin as possible.

A sound to my left pulled me up short. I stayed as still as I could and tried to control my breathing. It was silent. Too silent.

Some basic instinct kicked in and I ran again—leaving caution to fate. I ran almost blindly, as fast as I could. Branches scraped at me and pulled at my clothing, but I still didn't stop.

Inevitably, I tripped and fell again. The knife flew out of my hand, but I had no time to look for it. I was too desperate to flee. Climbing to my feet, I began to run as if my life depended on it, and I knew it did. Every fiber in my being told me I was being stalked, even though I'd seen no. The forest was deathly silent. All I heard was the noise I made and my own labored breathing.

In my frantic thoughts, I imagined Liam running with me, leading me to safety. I wondered if he knew I was missing. Would I die out here and never be found? The thought of never seeing Liam again caught me by surprise. I'm fighting for my very life and thinking about him, of all things. Not dying should be my only thought. Surprisingly, thinking about Liam gave me courage.

Without warning, I feel my feet leave the ground as I'm snatched up as if I weigh nothing. There's a moment of weightless and then it's gone as my back crashes onto the hard bed of pine needles. All the air leaves my lungs.

A dark face hovered above, and a firm hand held me to the ground. I couldn't breathe for several more moments, and my head felt foggy as I fought to stay conscious.

"There you are, Jessica. I was worried when I didn't find

you where I'd left you." I still couldn't make out the face, but there was no mistaking the voice. Lorenzo had found me.

Slowly, I managed to take shallow breaths as my body remembered how to breathe. Lorenzo easily lifted me from the ground. I was shaking uncontrollably, and it had nothing to do with the freezing temperatures.

"You almost ruined my plans," he said, pulling me in the direction I had been running. He had ahold of my leather jacket and held me against his body so that I was facing away from him. He reached around and grabbed my face, forcing me to look down.

At first, there were only murky shadows until my eyes adjusted enough to make out a cavernous valley, and I realized immediately that we were standing at the edge of a cliff. A cliff I almost ran over, if Lorenzo hadn't stopped me.

"Do you see? You almost died too soon," he said, his mouth next to my ear.

His words sent a new wave of fear through me. I wondered if I'd soon be wishing that I'd gone over the cliff.

BACK AT THE CABIN, I sat in a chair next to the fire. My hands weren't tied, but I didn't leave the chair. Lorenzo commanded me to sit, and I did. I wanted to sit but knew that it didn't make any sense.

I wanted to be running out the door, but I couldn't leave the chair. I began to do mini exercises by commanding my body to move. Slowly, but surely, I was getting the hang of it. The only thing was, it was exhausting to focus on telling each part of my body to obey me instead of this invisible compulsion.

Lorenzo was somewhere behind me, watching me. And then he was before me, looking down. My mind could barely register the speed in which he moved. I might have found him attractive under different circumstances. That made what he was all the more terrifying.

He smiled as if reading my mind. "You have no idea what I'm about to give you." He dropped to one knee and placed his hands on my thighs. The action was far too intimate, causing me to shudder.

"I don't want anything you have to offer," I spat.

He threw his head back and laughed. "That may be, but you'll change your mind soon."

"Never," I said, sounding braver than I felt.

"I'm going to make you like me, Jessica." My blood turned to ice.

"No," I breathed.

"I've grown tired of my adopted family and their silly rules. I plan to start my own family, beginning with you, my dear Jessica," he said, reaching up to tuck my hair behind one ear. The tender gesture made my skin crawl.

"No, I don't want this!" I said frantically.

"It's already begun. The initial bite was the first step," he said, still smiling his evil smile.

"The first bite?" I asked, my voice shaking.

"The night I came to visit. You remember?"

And I did. Suddenly, I could recall everything that happened during the hour I'd lost, and I was horrified. Not only at what Lorenzo had done to me, but at myself.

I remembered him standing on the porch. He told me to invite him in, and I did. He led me to the bedroom and closed the blinds. He walked around behind me and moved my hair aside, tilted my head and then...

He bit me! It hurt at first, but then it felt...good. I didn't want him to stop. It was sensual, and even though some dim notion in the far reaches of my mind knew what he was doing would eventually kill me, I didn't want it to end. I wondered if that was what addiction felt like.

I knew right where he bit me because it burned and pulsed, even now with the memory. I stared at him in horror. He brushed my lips with his thumb, and I turned my face away in shame.

"It takes three bites and then the first death. Then freedom as you've never known," he said, standing. I wasn't listening. I couldn't stop playing that moment in my head. How could I have let him? How could I have wanted it?

"How did you make me do that?" I asked, my voice trembling.

"It's a gift I have. We have many gifts, but only a few manifest, and then only certain ones receive certain gifts. Mine is persuasion, as you may have guessed. Only Victor and I have this particular gift," he said proudly.

"Who's Victor?" I asked, confused.

"Victor is the leader of my coven. Was. He'll be angry with me when he learns what I've done. You see, I've gone to a great deal of trouble to arrange this. I've been avoiding Victor and the rest of his lackeys, while also planning a way to steal you away from that guard dog of yours. Setting the fire was sheer brilliance. Wouldn't you agree?" I could only stare at him in shock and horror.

"You set that fire."

"You shouldn't look so surprised. I left you a pretty telling message with the lilies. You must've known I was coming for you," he said, feigning surprise. When I didn't answer, he added, "It doesn't matter. But this does," he said, then disappeared.

He was suddenly behind me, moving my hair from my neck. Every muscle in my body tightened, as my mind screamed at my body to flee.

Lorenzo slid my jacket off my shoulders. Underneath, I wore a loose sweater that hung almost off my shoulders, giving him complete access to my flesh. He held my arms as he gently kissed my exposed shoulders and then my neck in several places. His kisses became more demanding and rougher.

Then, I felt intense pain as his teeth sank into my neck. A scream escaped my lungs, filling the night with my terror.

22

*L*iam

We'd been triaged quickly and tucked into the back of a medic truck until the paperwork was completed. It was only a formality. We were ordered not to return to the fire as they currently had enough assistance.

I was anxious to get out of there and speak to Jessica. She may have still been on the scene, but I doubted it. I'd stop by her house first.

Seth was lying on the gurney with one arm draped over his eyes and the other hanging off the side. Cole and I sat on the benches generally used by the medics. Cole must have been bored because he was examining every drawer and cubby he could find.

We'd been discussing the fire and the fact that it was arson when Daisy poked her head in. I was surprised to see her. "Thank the heavens, I found you," she said, climbing into the back of the truck and pulling the two doors closed. She seemed anxious as she pushed Seth's legs over so she could sit on the gurney next to him.

Seth sat up, and Cole stopped poking around the rig.

"What's going on, Daisy? Where's Jessica?" A nervous feeling had started in my gut as soon as she closed the doors.

She looked at each of us in turn. Then she looked at me, and I could see the concern in her eyes. "That's why I'm here. Jess is missing," she said.

"What do you mean, she's missing?" I demanded.

Tears began to fill Daisy's eyes. "We were here, about to film. I went to the van for just a minute, then somehow the lights got unplugged, and she was just...gone," she said as she wiped at her face. "I told the sheriff, but he didn't seem to take it seriously. He said to call him if she's still not back by tomorrow evening."

She buried her head in Seth's chest, and he held her while I tried to think. "Daisy, what do you think happened to Jessica?" I asked, trying to gauge how much she knew.

"I'm afraid that Lorenzo guy took her. It's not like I could tell the sheriff that a dead guy took my best friend." She wiped her tears and looked up at me. "I know you think he's a vampire, so basically, you guys are all I've got. Who else would believe such a crazy idea?"

I turned to Cole and Seth. Their expressions were grave. "We have to find her. Let's divide up and try to find the other vampires. We can force one of them to lead us to Lorenzo," I said.

"What? There's more than one vampire?" Daisy said, sounding panicky.

I nodded.

"We're on it," Seth said. "I'll hit the hotel bar."

"I've got a few places in mind to check out. I'll keep you posted if I spot any," Cole said.

The doors started to open. The medic who had initially spoken to us looked at Daisy and then at us in confusion.

"Sorry. We have a family emergency to see to. If you can just sign off on our release, we'd appreciate it," I said, moving past him. Daisy, Seth, and Cole climbed out of the medic truck after me.

I could hear the paramedic stammering as we left. "But you haven't finished filling out the forms."

"We'll come back tomorrow," Cole promised.

Daisy insisted on staying with one of us, assuring me she could help, but we sent her home and promised to call her with updates if there were any. She reluctantly agreed.

We didn't know what could happen, and even though Daisy seemed to accept the existence of vampires, it didn't mean she wouldn't flip out if she knew what we were.

It was just before midnight, but the bars and restaurants were staying open late for all the visitors and locals celebrating Homecoming weekend.

I walked into the Moon and spotted Zoey drawing up a beer behind the bar. She made eye contact with me as I made my way toward her. I don't know if she saw something in my expression, but she finished serving the beer, then said something to the other bartender before coming to meet me.

She nodded for me to follow her. Zoey led me to the same employee hallway as before. As soon as she'd closed the door behind us, the noise was muffled.

"What's happened?" she asked warily.

"Jessica is missing. I think he took her," I said.

She knew who I meant because her expression looked frightened. "How long?" she asked.

"Sometime between seven and eight tonight," I said.

She leaned against the wall and seemed to be thinking hard. "It may be too late. You know that right?" she said, searching my eyes.

"I can't think about that. What do I need to do to find him and kill him, Zoey?"

She didn't answer right away. "I can do a locator spell that might point you in the right direction, but it's not always exact," she said cautiously.

I looked at her stunned. "What? Are you like a witch or something?"

Her gaze bored into me. "Ya think?" she said sarcastically.

I held my hands up in surrender. "I don't care. I just didn't know that was an actual thing," I confessed.

She raised an eyebrow at me. "Like you didn't know vampires were a thing? For shifters, you guys are pretty naïve."

"Exactly. We don't know why we're different, Zoey. But you saw that for yourself, didn't you?" I asked. She nodded. "When this is all over, I want to have a chat." I leaned back against the opposite wall, facing her. "Now, how do you do a locator spell, and how do I kill something that's technically already dead?"

I WAS on my way back from Jessica's house. Fortunately, Daisy was able to meet me there and let me in. She kept Jessica's spare keys. I could tell she wasn't comfortable allowing me into Jessica's home, especially when I asked for something personal of Jessica's.

"Do I want to know what this is for?" Daisy asked, when she came out of the bedroom, holding a necklace that belonged to Jessica.

"It's best if you don't," I said. I held out my hand, and she placed a small sapphire necklace into my palm.

"Let me know as soon as you find her," she said, locking the house as we left.

"I'll find her," I promised, before climbing into my truck. Daisy gave me a grateful smile, then got in her car. I pulled away from the curb and headed to Zoey's apartment above the bakery.

I'd only learned that she lived there tonight when she told me what she needed and where to meet her. I wasn't confident how to tell Cole that the woman he'd been crushing on for over a month was a practicing witch.

I wasn't even certain what that meant. Was it was a good thing, a bad thing, or did it even matter in the scheme of life? After all, Cole turned into a giant wolf. I guess we all had our issues.

I climbed the stairs to the top landing and the door opened before I could knock. Zoey stepped aside and motioned for me to enter. There were dozens of candles, and they were all lit, giving the apartment a warm but mysterious vibe.

Zoey pointed at a chair in front of a small table. The table was draped in a beaded silk shawl that a woman might wear. On the table sat one large copper bowl and one small ceramic bowl, along with several objects; dried plant clippings, and a white crystal fastened to a chain, and a few items I couldn't identify.

I sat where she indicated, and she took the opposite chair. There were three candles of different colors and heights placed around the edge of the larger bowl.

It looked like a confusing assortment of junk. "What's all of this?" I asked.

Zoey looked at me over the candle flames. She had pale skin with a splash of freckles across her nose and cheeks.

"Tools of the trade, you might say," she said, holding out her slender hand to me.

Her emerald-colored eyes were wide set and pretty, but

Zoey's most striking feature was her flaming red hair. It was beautiful, regardless if you preferred redheads or not.

I handed her the necklace. "This is hers? You're certain?" she asked, placing it in the ceramic bowl. I nodded.

She pulled something from her shirt pocket—a photo. Next, she took a pair of scissors and cut the picture and placed part of the photo in the ceramic bowl with the earrings. It was then that I realized the photo was of Jessica.

She must have been photographed with several others at the Burning Moon. Jessica was smiling and happy in the small image. I glanced up at Zoey.

"The picture will help direct the magic," she said, opening a small pocket knife that I hadn't noticed. "Give me your hand," she commanded.

I hesitantly offered her my left hand. Zoey held my index finger and ran the blade across it so fast, I didn't have time to question. She held fast to my finger and squeezed several drops of blood onto the photo. Hairs on the back of my neck tingled.

When she released my hand, I sucked on it to stop the bleeding. The cut would heal within minutes. She then drew the small knife across her own finger and did the same with her blood. I looked at her strangely.

"This is not the sort of magic I practice. It's considered dark magic or blood magic. My grandmother practiced the darker arts of witchcraft, so I picked up a few things, even though I grew up, not approving of her lifestyle. But this is the fastest and best way to do a locator spell when time is of the essence."

I wondered, now that I knew what Zoey was if she knew Cole liked her.

She lit a match and placed it in the bowl. There was nothing in the container to cause it to spark and flame, but it did. Zoey closed her eyes and said some words that I didn't understand.

When the flames died down, all that remained was purple ash. I'd never seen anything like it, but if it helped find Jessica, I'd go to hell and back. If that necklace had sentimental value, she might never speak to me again, but I was willing to pay that price too.

Zoey began collecting everything from the table and placing it in the copper bowl. She then set it aside, on the kitchen counter. She spread a map of Flagstaff onto the table.

Zoey took the ash from the bowl and scattered it on top of the map. I watched, curious about the process, but also wondering if this was just a bunch of parlor tricks and a waste of time.

She dangled a crystal hanging from a chain, out over the map. When she closed her eyes again, her hair blew softly in a breeze that wasn't there. I felt nothing but a tingling up and down my spine.

The crystal began to move of its own accord, as far as I could tell. And the ash on the map started to rustle and move as if by the phantom wind. It moved and gathered over a forested area west of town.

Finally, the crystal and the ash stopped moving, and so did Zoey's hair. She let out a long sigh and shook her head.

"What happened?" I demanded.

"I'm sorry. It isn't giving me enough. The area is too large. She's in the forest, but the area is too vast to do you much good. It could take a week to search that much area," Zoey said, looking sad and defeated.

"That can't be it. Try again," I said, offering her my hand.

She gave me a sad look. "It won't work. I'm sorry that I couldn't do better."

"I'll find her," I said, knowing it was still a long shot.

My phone buzzed, and I pulled it out of my pocket. It was Seth.

"Yes?"

"I got something. Meet me in front of the Weatherford hotel," Seth said.

I looked at Zoey. "I'll be right there. I'm just down the street at Zoey's."

"Zoey's?" Seth sounded surprised.

"I'll tell you about it later," I said and ended the call.

"Good news, I hope?" Zoey asked.

"I hope so," I said, turning for the door. I paused at the door and turned back. "Thank you, Zoey." She smiled softly.

"Liam."

"Yes?"

"Your bite is deadly to a vampire, but only in your other form. It's the only chance you have to kill him," Zoey said. "Good luck."

I nodded, then left to meet Seth.

*C*ole and Seth were standing on the sidewalk in front of the old hotel. So were the two vampires I'd met the night before. I came to a stop in front of my brothers. "What've you got?"

Seth handed me a map. It was the same local map Zoey had used. The one tourists purchased in almost every shop in town.

"What's this?" I asked, unfolding it. I glanced at Olivia and Simon. Both were glancing around nervously.

"Should we take this inside?" I asked.

Olivia nodded, so I led us into the hotel lobby. I finished opening the map and saw a small X that marked a spot within the area where the purple ash had settled on Zoey's map.

I looked at Seth, who nodded toward Olivia. Now that we were off the street, Olivia's cool attitude had returned. She stared at me defiantly.

"Is this where he's taken her?" I asked.

"I suspected this location because I followed him there once. Simon confirmed that the blonde is there. Lorenzo almost caught him." She smiled at her companion. "But Simon's too smart and too fast for Lorenzo." Simon shrugged at her compliment.

"Why would you help us?" Cole asked, giving voice to my own thoughts.

Olivia looked at Seth. "Do with it what you want. It's not my concern. Maybe it's a peace offering," she said, looking bored.

"You speak for the other vampires?" I asked.

She seemed to bristle at my suggestion, and stepped toward me, glaring defiantly. She couldn't have been over five-four and a hundred and ten pounds soaking wet. But she didn't seem to notice our size difference, or she didn't care.

"I speak for myself." She rolled her small shoulders and stepped back. "I don't care about the other leeches. Like I said. Do with it what you want."

"We're supposed to believe that?" Cole said, stepping forward. Simon, who I'd never heard say a word, stepped forward to meet Cole. Simon was in Cole's face, green eyes flashing.

"Easy, you two. We're trying to work together here," Seth said, moving closer to the two men with his hands raised in a passive manner.

"Speak for yourself," Cole said acidly.

"It's all right, Simon," Olivia said, placing a hand on his shoulder. "They don't trust us yet."

Cole looked ready to rumble. Simon loosened some of the tension in his body and stepped back.

"Cole," I warned.

Cole stepped back and relaxed his posture, somewhat.

"We don't have time for this," I said. "I know this area. Am I looking for anything in particular?"

"It's a small building or cabin in the woods. I think hunters use it," Olivia said, pulling Simon away from us. "I'd hurry. If he were just going to kill her, he wouldn't have gone to all this trouble. You'd have found her body by now," she said as she and Simon walked away.

"Wait," I said. Olivia and Simon stopped and turned around. "Is Lorenzo the leader who brought you here?"

Olivia cracked up laughing, and Simon smiled for the first time. "Yeah, right. Victor is the head of our coven. Lorenzo can't tell his head from his ass. Nobody would follow that loser. His own people were going to off him before he convinced Victor to turn him," Olivia said, now in better humor.

"Should we be concerned about the rest of your family?" I asked.

Olivia cocked her head to the side. "Like what?" she asked.

"Like more people dying?" Cole spat.

She looked at us for a moment.

"Olivia," Simon said, surprising us all. He sounded Jamaican.

"Oh, it's all right, Simon. I won't share all our secrets." She smiled at us and winked at Simon. "I wouldn't go so far as to say that they aren't killers, but they prefer to be more discreet when they eat." Olivia was enjoying the impact her words were having.

"Meaning?" Seth asked.

"Meaning, they leave a beating heart. Does that help you sleep better at night?" she asked.

"Does it help you sleep better?" Cole countered. I could tell that he'd gotten to her.

"You don't know anything about me, so don't pretend that you do," Olivia said, then turned on her heels to leave. Simon gave us one last look, then followed her out.

None of this sounded good. So, who was this Victor, and how dangerous was he? I didn't trust Olivia, but I had no choice at this point. I needed to find Jessica. An over-whelming feeling of fear washed over me, and I sucked in a deep breath.

"What's wrong?" Seth asked.

I didn't understand the feeling, but I had a clear vision of Jessica, and I could almost hear her scream in the back of my mind.

"It's Jessica. We need to move fast," I said. "I need one of you here, in case this is a trap."

I opened the map one more time. "Cole, you stay and keep your eyes open. Seth, I want you in the forest with me. We have to shift if we want to kill him."

"Why is that?" Seth asked.

"Something about our bite is fatal to vampires," I said.

"Where'd you learn something like that?" Cole asked suspiciously.

"Zoey told me," I said, seeing the surprise cross his face. "We'll talk about that later. Seth, we gotta move now."

"What're you waiting for, big brother? Let's go save your girl," Seth said, motioning me toward the door.

When we reached my truck, I gave Cole a quick hug. I didn't want to pretend that I knew what was going to happen tonight. And if I was leaving my youngest brother on his own, I wanted him to know I cared.

Cole welcomed the embrace and squeezed me tight before letting go and slapping me on the arm.

Seth didn't bother with any hugs, choosing to yell at us from inside the truck, instead. "Let's go already. We'll be back soon, Cole. You can count on it."

Cole and I grinned at Seth's confidence. "He's right, of course," I reassured Cole, then climbed behind the wheel.

We drove away without any more fuss. Cole was standing under the streetlamp in the road, with his hands in his pockets, watching us go. He was still standing there when we turned at the next block until I could no longer see him.

———————

WE DROVE in silence most of the way. I was doing ninety, which was as fast as my old truck could go. It took us thirty minutes to reach the forest service road that would take us closer to the area Jessica was being held. It was another twenty after that point.

I was hoping that Olivia's information was reliable. It was possible that there was a rift within their ranks, but I wouldn't know for sure until we found Jessica. Win or lose, I was laying it all on the table.

"This is the spot," I said when we arrived at a gate in the road. We could have broken the lock and continued driving, but we planned to shift to cover more ground. Since we had only flashes of memory once we changed, it was a gamble that we'd continue our search for Jessica.

I felt strongly that even after I shifted, my wolf wanted to find Jessica as much as I did. Since I was the alpha, my goals would be Seth's goals.

"Remember to think about finding Jessica when you shift," I told Seth.

"Already on it," he said, climbing out of the truck.

I could see our breath once we exited the warmth of the vehicle. Seth began stripping off his clothes without hesitation.

I couldn't help but worry about risking my brother's life and exposing our secret. I just hoped we weren't too late. It had been over five hours since she was taken.

When I was done pulling off my clothes, Seth was already a large black wolf that blended into the night. Only his eyes glowed amber in the darkness. He barked at me, and I nodded. He turned and ran into the woods.

When I was naked, I placed my clothes on the seat of the truck and hid the keys under the wheel. I closed my eyes and embraced the animal always just below the surface of my human skin. It no longer hurt, as it did in the beginning. I learned quickly to stop resisting and to just let go.

I did that now, and in one magical fluid movement, I was a large, powerful creature on the hunt. Trees blurred by as I picked up speed. There was a scent or two I was searching for, and that was all I knew at the moment.

One was the scent of something dead but not dead. The other was that of my mate. Either smell would lead me to the other. But it was her smell that I caught first.

I picked up speed, and the scent grew stronger and stronger. I was close. Another smell warned me to slow my pace. Smoke lingered on the air, and that too was becoming stronger.

A small shack came into view. I knew instinctively that she was there. I threw my head back and howled loudly into the night—a cry to tell her I was coming for her. I heard one of my pack respond with his own call, but he was far away.

We were stronger together, but I couldn't wait for him. She needed my protection.

24

*J*essica

When I woke, I felt weak and sick. For several minutes I couldn't open my eyes. It took too much effort. Something deep within me knew I had to get up. It was imperative that I escape, but at that moment, my head was so foggy, I couldn't remember why.

It took a great effort to open my eyes. My body felt like a heavy weight rested on me, preventing my limbs from moving. The first thing I saw was the bear's head, and I remembered where I was and why.

I had a new resolve and forced my head to turn and study the room. Lorenzo was leaning against the wall, next to the fire watching me with a satisfied gleam in his eyes.

He'd bitten me twice. He meant to do it again. And then what? He'd kill me, and I'd be like him? I couldn't let that happen. There had to be a way out. *Think, Jess, think.*

The only weapon I had was somewhere in the forest, and of no use to me now. As I watched, Lorenzo pushed away from the wall and moved to the side of the cot where I was lying. He gazed down at me.

"You're awake. I thought I'd be waiting until tomorrow," he said, reaching down and pulling me up like a rag doll. He held me easily in his arms, but seeing my lack of resistance, he seemed to reconsider.

He sat on the cot and steadied me until I managed to hold myself up. Some of my strength was returning, but it was a slow process, and I wondered if I could even make it to full speed without a hospital to replenish the blood he'd already taken.

I struggled to stay upright and awake. Lorenzo brought a chair over and sat in it. He watched me. "You know, I think I could finish this now," he said with enthusiasm. "I've never done this before. You'll be my first."

"Why are you doing this to me?" I managed weakly.

"You don't understand now, but you will. I knew when I saw you in the bar with those dogs. You were a woman who could hold her own. I chose you, then and there, to be my mate, to be my equal." Lorenzo leaned over and kissed me on the lips. It was a long, lingering kiss, but I had only enough fight in me to stay awake.

I'd already decided to reserve my strength in case an opportunity presented itself. Resisting his kiss would have taken too much of my energy. Fighting him now would not serve me in the end.

I decided that it might be possible to distract him. It could buy me some time. "How did you become a vampire?" I asked.

He looked genuinely excited by my question. "That's an interesting tale. I was a businessman in the nineties—very successful, I might add. I had a falling out with one of my business associates, and well…he tended to hold a grudge." Lorenzo seemed happy to weave his story for me, so I pretended to listen while I tried to think of a way out.

"This business associate ordered a hit on me, so I went

underground for a while. That's when I discovered Victor, and quite by chance discovered what he was. I propositioned him to turn me, and he did. I later went back and took revenge on the associate who wanted me dead by killing his entire family," he said, smiling as if he'd remembered a fond moment.

I hadn't believed I could be any more frightened, but I was wrong.

"So, why do you want to leave Victor then?" I asked, feigning a weak interest.

I could tell that my attention pleased him. "I've grown tired of Victor and his weak ways. I've learned all that he can teach me, and now he just holds me back. I prefer to feast where he would rather dine if you get my meaning."

"What are you going to do now?" I asked.

He surprised me by kissing me again. And again, I didn't resist. Conserving my strength for one final battle was my only priority.

When he pulled away, he seemed pleased by my lack of resistance. I merely watched him cautiously. He moved from his chair to sit next to me on the cot.

I fought the urge to recoil. He slipped an arm around my back and moved my hair away from my neck as he'd done before. My heart raced, and a feeling of panic rushed through me.

He's going to bite me.

My mind fumbled with what to do, as his lips grazed my collarbone and traveled up my neck. I tensed, ready to spend whatever strength I had left to fight him—even knowing it was a futile effort.

And then I heard it.

A wolf howled in the distance, and I thought of my dreams. Another wolf answered the call, but it was faint and hard to hear. How I wish I was with them now.

Lorenzo also heard the wolves. He paused with his lips on my neck and stiffened. His head turned from me, and he listened intently. It seemed almost humorous that he was concerned by some wolves or coyotes howling in the forest.

But he was concerned. I could see it in his mannerisms. He got up from the cot to peer out the windows, one by one. Lorenzo was...frightened. This made no sense, but it diverted his attention from me, and that was a good thing.

A wolf howled again, and this time the sound was much closer. It even gave me chills. There was something familiar in the cry. It made me think of my recent dream. That was an excellent thought to have if this were to be my last moments. I'd hold on to the image.

When Lorenzo heard the wolf again, he cursed and went to the door. He opened it and peered outside. I used this moment to try to stand, using the help of the chair and the wall.

Lorenzo stepped outside, and I held onto the wall for stability, trying to make it to the fireplace. Next to the hearth was a metal poker for the fire. It was the only weapon I could think of. I just had to reach it, but it meant passing the door that Lorenzo went through.

I heard growling from outside and hesitated. It was so loud, it must have been right outside the cabin. The poker was another fifteen feet away and the amount of energy I'd used just to get halfway across the small room was over-whelming.

Something was happening outside, but I dared not stop to find out. Reaching the fireplace and the poker was all I could focus on. Sounds of a struggle were coming from beyond the door.

I imagined two wild animals locked in a ferocious battle. I had my own struggle—drag myself to the fireplace. With the poker, at least I could go down fighting.

An animal yelped in pain, and I stumbled. My heart ached for the beast, and I hoped Lorenzo hadn't hurt it. I crawled the rest of the way until I reached the hearth and wrapped my fingers around the poker. I looked over my shoulder, but nobody had come through the open door.

Lorenzo cursed as sounds of a violent struggle continued. I used the poker to help me rise to my feet. I could see only darkness beyond the opened door.

I slowly made my way over to the door and peered outside. If I'd had more strength, I'd already have escaped through the back door. No, it was stand and fight or lay down and die. I wouldn't survive another long run in the woods.

Nervously, I peered out the door and tried to focus my eyes on the moving shadows. It was difficult, but as my vision adjusted, I saw an enormous wolf. I gasped and my heart skipped a beat as I clung to the doorway. The wolf and Lorenzo were circling one another. Both looked tired and wary.

There was something dark on the wolf's light coat, and I feared it was blood. I'd never seen a wolf this large. And where was its pack?

Lorenzo didn't look much better. His silk shirt hung in tatters on his shoulders, and long bloody scratches marked his arms, chest, and back. And that perfectly slicked-back hair was a mess, hanging in his eyes.

The more clearly I could see the wolf, the more convinced I was that this was the one from my dream. I felt an affinity to the wolf—bound to it, but I didn't know how or why. It was just a feeling.

In a vicious move, Lorenzo feigned to his left but attacked on the right. The wolf was caught off guard just long enough for Lorenzo to grab the great beast around its chest.

I could see Lorenzo's muscles straining as he squeezed.

He was crushing the animal's chest. I couldn't let that happen. Stumbling out the door, I drew close to him. Lorenzo was so intent on killing the wolf that he didn't notice me until it was too late.

I pulled the poker back like I used to hold a bat during softball. The wolf was fading, but our eyes met briefly. It seemed to me that the wolf's eyes held sadness when it looked at me. My resolve doubled, as I swung the poker at Lorenzo's head with every ounce of my fading strength.

My attack wasn't anything to write home about. It didn't even seem to hurt Lorenzo, but it did catch him off guard for an instant. His grip loosened, just enough.

I fell to the ground with my effort and scrambled backwards as quickly as I could. The moment Lorenzo cried out in frustration, the wolf jerked its body and broke free of the vampire's grasp.

As it did, the wolf sank its powerful jaws into Lorenzo's arm. The vampire reacted with a blood-curdling screech as he backhanded the wolf, sending the great beast hurtling through the air and into the trunk of a big tree. The wolf yelped as it hit the tree and I screamed.

At the base of the tree, the wolf's body lay still. Lorenzo was staring at his arm in horror as dark smoke started pouring from the wounds as if he'd sprung a leak. He screeched an inhuman sound and vanished so fast into the forest that I would have sworn he'd disappeared if not for the branches that were still moving from his departure.

The wolf still hadn't moved. I realized I was crying. Cautiously, I eased closer to the wolf. My heart was racing. I'd almost reached the animal when another wolf, came out of the trees. This wolf was almost as large as the first one, but jet black.

I froze. The wolf looked at me, then at the lifeless wolf a few feet away. It threw its head back, howling loud and long.

I still hadn't moved a muscle. I was too afraid. Then the wolf looked at me again and whimpered. It was such a sad sound my heart hurt.

The black wolf began walking closer to me, and I found that I couldn't move. I was frozen to the spot. It stood directly in front of me and whined again. It looked over to the other wolf, and I cautiously pulled my gaze away to see the other wolf.

I gasped. A man was lying still as death, right where the wolf had been. And he was completely naked. "What the—"

I looked from the man, back to the black wolf, but it was gone. Scared out of my mind, I moved closer to the man and cautiously bent down to see his face. Shocked beyond reason, I stumbling back, falling on my butt and then crab-walked back further still.

The man was Liam.

After the initial shock subsided enough that I could breathe again, I moved close enough to touch him. I felt for a pulse in his throat and found one. I sighed in relief. There were no apparent injuries and no blood. I prayed that he would be all right.

I made my way into the cabin on wobbly legs but managed to pull down one of the Indian blankets covering the windows and returned to place it over Liam. The sun was just beginning to brighten the sky but hadn't risen over the mountains yet.

It was freezing cold, but I hadn't noticed until now. Adrenaline was a beautiful thing. I sat next to him and watched him breathe. Leaving him was out of the question, and he was too heavy for me to get him into the cabin. So, I sat there staring at him in wonder.

I don't know how much time passed before a truck, that I recognized as Liam's, pulled up. It came to a stop in front of the cabin and Seth got out. He didn't seem surprised to see me or overly concerned that his brother was unconscious, and obviously naked under the flimsy blanket —facts that made me suspicious of his timely arrival.

My head was still foggy from blood loss, but I know something extraordinary happened here in the early morning hours, and it wasn't merely the vampire.

Seth looked at Liam, and then at me. He looked concerned, but I had the feeling it had nothing to do with the obvious. "Are you okay?" he asked, taking his coat off and putting it around me. Then he sat down next to me on the ground.

"I don't know, but I'm worried about Liam," I said, studying his face. "Why don't you look worried, Seth?" I asked.

He searched my face. "Liam will be fine. But you need to get to a hospital. You're pale as a ghost, and I think you're going into shock," he said.

"Is that how you'll explain the things I've seen?" I asked, holding his gaze.

Quietly, he said, "We won't be here to hear your explanation. Much less give our own."

At first, I didn't understand what he meant, but then I read the meaning on his face. They were leaving. I knew Liam's secret and that was enough for them to flee. "Why? Why leave? This is your home."

"Because some secrets are too dangerous to make the evening news, Jessica," Seth said. He looked away and ran his hand through his dark hair that was so different from Liam, and Cole's lighter coloring. He looked sad, and maybe tired.

"What if I don't tell anyone?" I asked, my heart aching at the thought of never seeing Liam again.

"You're a reporter, it's your job. What journalist would pass up a story like that? I don't blame you. None of us do. Liam knew it was a risk to get involved with you, but some things can't be ignored," Seth said, his typical good humor returning as he smiled at me. "And Liam couldn't ignore you if he tried. And he did," he laughed.

I couldn't return his smile. Too many troubling thoughts crowded my mind. That's when I knew I was going to pass out. The blood loss, the adrenaline surges, the cold. My body couldn't take any more as my head swayed and my vision blurred, then…lights out.

*L*iam

I'd been packing up essentials all day. Everything else would be left behind. We'd leave with everything we arrived with eight years ago. I'd have new memories and a few more regrets than when I came, but that was the way it had to be.

Cole and Seth had left earlier to do the same. It made me feel like a failure, and I tried to look back on the last week and figure out what I could have done differently, but it all kept turning out the same in my mind.

Any scenario with her could only end badly. Jessica was the worst person I could fall for, and the only person I could fall for. Conceding that fact didn't make it any easier to walk away from her. This was infinitely harder than the last time.

We hadn't decided where to go, but we figured we'd try Colorado or Oregon first. I'd already contacted the attorney who handled our finances and secured documentation for us the first time we disappeared. He was a handy man to have on speed-dial, though I'd hoped to not need his services for something like this ever again.

It felt strange to learn that Jessica knew my secret. When I came to, I was here in my bed, and Cole and Seth were drinking coffee out front. They told me what had happened, and we all knew what that meant.

The vampire almost killed me. It had never taken that long to regenerate from an injury. Seth said that Cole brought me home, while he took Jessica to the hospital. She was stable and would most likely be released in the morning.

It was all I could do not to go to her. Even though I suspected she wouldn't want to see me. Seth said she was calm about what had happened, but he also thought her reaction may have been because of shock.

If what Zoey told me about our bite being fatal for vampires was true, Lorenzo wouldn't be a threat to Jessica or anyone else ever again. And that was worth it. Thoughts of Jessica filled my head the entire day. I figured that we only had a couple of days before the word would get out and we'd be facing questions we couldn't answer.

That would have to be enough time to settle our affairs while leaving others hanging. I'd write letters of resignation for all of us and leave them at the station for the chief to discover.

I was in the middle of pounding a For Sale sign in the ground when I recognized Daisy's car coming down my gravel drive. I walked over warily, and she stepped out of the car.

"Hey, Liam. You doing okay?" she asked. Daisy shouldn't have been concerned about me.

"I'm good. How's Jessica?" I asked, genuinely wanting to know.

"She's doing great, thanks to you," she said, beaming at me.

"Did you drive all the way out here to ask how I was?"

Daisy looked unsure as she fidgeted about, by first

tucking her hands in her pockets and then taking them out and crossing them over her chest, and finally deciding to let them hang by her sides.

"No. I came for Jess," she said.

I waited, feeling anxious at the mention of her name.

"I mean, she asked me to talk to you." She still looked uncomfortable.

"About what?"

She pushed her glasses higher onto her nose. "She wants you to stay. At least until she can talk to you," Daisy said.

My gut tightened, and anger colored my words. "I'm not doing an interview, Daisy, so forget it."

"No, no! That's not what she wants. It's not about that. She has something she wants to tell you, but if you run away, Jessica won't be able to tell you," she pleaded.

"I'm not running away," I growled.

Daisy tipped her head to the side and looked at me. "Then what do you call it?" she asked.

I thought about that for a moment. Maybe she was right. Perhaps I was running away. Cole had accused me of that when I left Harmony. In a softer tone, I said, "It's the only way. What do you know about it, anyway?"

She smiled then. "I know that you, and maybe Cole and Seth, are different, and that's okay. I know that in a world of broken hearts, lonely people, and missed opportunities, that you and Jess have some sort of chemistry that's worth exploring." She paused for a moment.

"And, I know that there are things in this world that I don't understand, and maybe I don't need to understand. But what I know for certain is this town needs heroes like Cole, Seth, and you."

She seemed sincere when she walked over to me and stood on her toes to kiss my cheek. I smiled in spite of myself. She walked back to her car. When she opened the door, she looked back at me. "Don't leave without talking to her. You may be safer, but nobody ever conquered anything by staying safe." Daisy winked at me, got into the car and drove away.

I THOUGHT about Daisy's suggestion for most of the day. There was nothing I wanted more than to believe there was a chance that I could stay close to Jessica, even if it was at a distance.

But my head wouldn't allow my heart to make the hard decision. The weather called for rain the next few days, so I was securing a waterproof tarp over the items I'd packed in the bed of the truck.

I couldn't have timed it better, because the rain had just begun to hit when I went inside and opened a beer. I turned on the news, thinking of Jessica, but dreading the thought of seeing our pictures flash across a breaking news story.

So far, there'd been no mention of anything except the fire at the university. It still hadn't been ruled an act of arson, but those things took time—just like ruling a death as a homicide.

Thankfully, the two victims we pulled from the fire were expected to make a full recovery. They were still being treated for smoke inhalation.

The rain pounded the fiberglass walls of the fifth wheel trailer that I called home. Cole, Seth, and I would call it home until we figured things out.

An urgent knock sounded on the door, startling me out of my daydream. I moved the curtain aside to see Jessica was holding her coat over her head, and it did nothing to keep the rain off her. I opened the door and pulled her inside--out of the storm.

Jessica was breathing hard, her breasts straining against her wet blouse as she pushed her damp hair away from her face. Her complexion was pale, and her eyes looked tired. She should have been in the hospital. But she was still breathtakingly beautiful. A large bandage on her neck looked out of place.

Seeing it made me glad I'd bitten the vampire who dared to touch her. When she noticed me looking at her neck, she nervously moved her hand to cover it.

"What are you doing out of the hospital? " I asked, not meaning to sound angry, but it may have come out that way. I was worried about her, but it didn't translate in my voice.

She didn't seem to notice. Instead, she smiled and extended her hand. I looked at her hand and then back up to her eyes, confused.

"I want to start over. We met under terrible circumstances, and some awful things have happened since that day." She blushed under my gaze. It only made me want her more. "What I'm trying to say, is can we start over, like normal people meeting for the first time?" she asked.

"What if one of us isn't normal?" I asked, nervous to hear her reply.

"Normal is overrated," she whispered. That made me smile.

I reached for her hand. "I'm Liam McKenzie, it's a pleasure to meet you," I said, holding her hand.

She smiled. "I'm Jessica Parker. So, Liam McKenzie, I was wondering if you'd like to have dinner with me next week," she said, then bit her lower lip.

It was her unspoken question that hung in the air—*would I still be here next week. "I don't know if that's possible."*

As if reading my thoughts, she said, "I know you're planning to leave. If the For Sale sign outside didn't clue me in, Seth told me...while you were unconscious." Her pale cheeks turned red, and she looked away. "I know that I'm the reason. I thought that maybe if you got to know me better, you'd decide that I was someone you could trust...rather than someone who'd do anything for a story." She turned her gaze on me now.

"I want to trust you. You don't know how badly I want that," I said. She moved closer to me.

"Then say yes," she said softly. I closed the distance between us. We were so close her head tipped back to stare up at me.

As if a magnet were pulling us together, I lowered my head and kissed her. This kiss was filled with so many things I think we both wanted to say but hadn't had the opportunity. Daisy's words came to mind—*missed opportunities.*

I didn't want to miss anything with this woman, even if it was fleeting and temporary, because I knew she had big plans that I wouldn't fit into. Whatever time I could steal with her, I'd gladly take it.

Her wet clothes soaked into my shirt and jeans. I suddenly remembered she was just in the hospital and pulled back, holding her at arm's length. "Why aren't you at the hospital?" I asked, my voice husky with desire.

She reached up and touched my rough, unshaven cheek. "I was afraid you'd leave before I saw you. It was a risk I didn't want to take, so I checked myself out of the hospital— against doctor's orders," she confessed, with a sly smile.

"I'm taking you back. First, you need some dry clothes." I left her standing there to fetch something of mine she could wear. I returned with a red flannel shirt and a pair of straight-legged jogging pants with an elastic waistband and drawstring.

When I returned, I found her looking around the small trailer with open curiosity. She picked up a picture of my parents and studied it. She looked at me. "Are these your parents?" I nodded. "Where are they?"

"They've passed. Within a year of each other," I said.

She looked sad. "I'm sorry. I shouldn't have been so nosy."

I took the picture from her and looked at the smiling faces of my adopted parents. I still missed them and thought about them each and every day. Sometimes I thought about my birth mother that I never knew.

"It's okay. It's been eight years," I said, placing the picture back on the shelf.

"They aren't designer, but they'll keep you warm," I said, handing her the clothes.

She took them and looked behind me at the small hallway. "The bathroom's tiny. You can change in my room at the end. I put a towel on the bed," I said, sitting down on the built-in sofa.

"Thank you," she said shyly, then went in the room and pulled the divider closed.

JESSICA NODDED off against my shoulder on the way back to the hospital. I drove her car to the hospital. I'd catch a ride home from one of my brothers. We arrived at the hospital, and they admitted her right away.

I had to admit, Jessica looked mighty cute in my running pants and a flannel shirt. She'd tied the flannel in a knot, but she was still swimming in my clothes. Once she was in a room, they let me come to see her. I'd made a quick stop at the hospital gift shop and purchased a small vase of flowers for her.

When I entered the room, she smiled at the arrangement. "Are those for me?"

"No, they're for your nurse," I said, winking at the older woman as she walked past me.

The woman giggled. "Oh, he's a charmer. You better keep that one," she said, as she left the room.

I put the flowers on the table next to the bed. "Thank you," Jessica said.

"What time?" I asked.

She blinked at me. "What?"

"What time are you taking me to dinner next week?" I said, grinning.

She laughed and tapped her lips like she was thinking. "How about Friday, at six?"

"It's a date," I said.

"Does this mean you'll stay?" she asked, the playfulness gone.

"At least long enough to cash in on that dinner," I said, leaning down to tuck a piece of her hair behind her ear.

"That'll do for now. I didn't want to go to sleep and wake up to learn you'd left," she said, closing her eyes and relaxing into the pillow.

I took that as my cue to leave. I bent down and kissed her head softly.

I was almost out of the room when I heard her say, "Thank you, Liam."

I turned around. "For what?"

"For saving my life," she said, her eyes still closed. I smiled to myself.

"Get some rest," I said, then left the hospital, feeling hopeful for the first time in a long time.

26

*J*essica

This was the busiest and most challenging week of my life. Not to mention, the last two weeks had been life-changing.

"Are you almost done?" Daisy complained. I finished applying the most basic amount of makeup to her eyes.

Daisy had a flawless complexion, stunning light brown eyes, and a lovely face. She was a knockout, but it was easy to miss behind her large, black-rimmed glasses. Tonight she wore contacts and a cute black cocktail dress that showed off the figure nobody knew she had.

I stepped back to admire my handiwork and almost didn't recognize my best friend. The result was all Daisy, just uncovered. I'd barely given her a little color on her lids, mascara, and a dab of lip gloss. She was a natural beauty. I couldn't help but smile, which seemed to annoy her.

"Now I'm done," I said.

"You better not have made me look like a clown, or I'm washing my face," she grumbled.

"Look for yourself," I encouraged, looking toward the mirror.

Daisy slowly turned to look at her reflection. She stared for several moments with her lips parted.

Her lack of response made me worried she hated it but, how could she?

"What did you do?" she asked quietly.

She hated it. "I'm sorry. I think you look beautiful. I can take off the shadow," I said, reaching for a makeup wipe.

"So do I," she said, and I stopped mid-reach to look at her. She was smiling at herself in the mirror. "How did you make me look so good?" she asked, sounding astonished.

I laughed then. "Daisy, this is all you. You barely have any makeup on. It doesn't get much more *el natural* than this." I bent down and put my hands on her shoulders and my head next to hers. "You're simply beautiful. Don't hide it or fear it," I said.

She turned and beamed at me. "Thank you. I'm so glad you didn't listen to me." Daisy stood and twirled in front of a full-length mirror in my bedroom. "I can't believe I have a date with Eric Chambers."

"Ha, Eric is lucky to have a date with you. He won't know what hit him. Besides, it wasn't like I had to twist his arm. He seemed surprised when I mentioned you were single and had commented on how handsome you thought he was. He asked for your number right away," I said, smirking.

"Are you sure you didn't have to pay him?" Daisy joked.

"I bet he would have paid me. Maybe I should have asked for a finder's fee," I said, laughing.

"That would make you my pimp," Daisy said, grinning.

I picked up the long, felt coat I was loaning her for the evening. Daisy only owned leather and flannel. After I helped her into the jacket, I walked her to the front door. She was meeting Eric at a local bar and restaurant for dinner and drinks.

Daisy was a little wobbly in heels, but at least she owned a pair. She would have been swimming in my size nine shoes. She walked to her car, at times looking like a fashion model or maybe a baby deer learning to walk. She stopped just before she got into the car. "I almost forgot! Good luck tonight. Let me know how everything goes with Liam," she said.

I waved and closed the door. Liam would be here in thirty minutes, and I wasn't even close to being ready. I'd gotten so caught up in Daisy's date preparations, I'd neglected my own.

As I hurriedly touched up my makeup and changed clothes, I thought about the crazy things that had happened since I first got the call about the two campers.

I'd had no idea how that one terrible situation was going to change my life in so many ways. I suspected the origins of the story could have catapulted my career, but I'd never have imagined the course I'd be on today.

The experiences over the last couple of weeks reminded me that life wasn't to be taken for granted. I also realized that the path I was following with blind determination wasn't the direction that I wanted my life to go.

It took almost dying to make me recognize what I really wanted, and what I really wanted had always taken a sideline to what my parents thought, and what I felt was the safer path. But sometimes life wasn't safe. Sometimes, we needed to take chances.

A knock at the front door reminded me of the other thing I wanted and needed in my life. I opened the door to find Liam standing in my doorway wearing a corduroy blazer, a denim collared shirt, and a sexy smile.

I hadn't seen him since that day at the hospital. I'd kept him at arm's length for a good reason. I wanted to sort some things out in my life and be one hundred percent certain of the changes I was making before starting something with Liam.

We'd talked on the phone several times when he'd called to see how I was doing. I recovered quickly and got busy with the plan I'd decided on while I'd recovered in the hospital.

"Hi," I said, smiling.

"Hi." He stood there, smiling but also looking nervous.

I stepped aside to let him enter. He was almost too big for my tiny home. "I had planned to make you dinner, but something unexpected came up, so I ordered from Angelo's. I hope you like Italian," I said.

"That's one of my favorites," he said.

I was nervous about sharing my news with Liam. Would he be happy for me? Would he react like my parents and think I was on drugs? There was something in his eyes that made me feel he'd always support me. I motioned for him to take a seat at the kitchen table.

He noticed the white linen tablecloth and the two candles I'd lit and smiled at me.

"I have something to tell you," I said. His smile faded, and I could see the tension in the veins on his neck and the way his body tightened. "It's not bad. I'm hoping you won't think I'm crazy," I said quickly.

"You're here with me, so maybe you're a little crazy," he said, sounding serious.

"I'm not afraid of you, Liam McKenzie." I reached across the table and placed my hand on his.

He looked at my hand and then back to my eyes. "Maybe you should be."

I kept my gaze steady. "I'm not. You won't hurt me, Liam."

"How can you be sure, when I'm not?" he asked, his eyes hard but also searching.

"I just know. I can't explain it, but I know you'd never hurt me. I'm certain, even if you're not."

"I would never want to hurt you or anyone else, but we don't understand ourselves or why we're this way. I don't have all the answers, and the idea of putting you at risk is the worst feeling I can think of," he said.

"I have something to show you after dinner," I said.

"Show me?" Liam asked, with a mischievous grin that made my heart beat fast.

I rolled my eyes at him. "You'll see," I said, and winked at him.

FOOD WAS DELIVERED, and we talked through the meal about our families, growing up, and even touched on politics. It was light, friendly, and flirty banter. And surprisingly easy. Talking to Liam was natural and comfortable, like pulling on a favorite sweater. I saw a side of him that was unguarded and open, and I loved every moment of it.

When we finished, he held my hand as we walked to his truck. Liam opened the door for me and helped me up into the cab. I'd worn a dress and heels because tonight was important to me. Maybe it would be to Liam as well.

I directed him where to go, leading him into the older downtown area that I felt was the heart of Flagstaff and rich with the town's history. We parked on a corner and walked a block down the street. We passed the bakery, and I noticed we both glanced up at Zoey's apartment.

Liam had told me that she was helpful in locating me, and between her and the rogue vampires named Olivia and Simon, he was able to find me. I shivered, thinking that if Liam had been a few minutes later, I'd be dead or a vampire.

It was still hard to believe that there were more of them

living in Flagstaff now. I wasn't sure how the town would be big enough for them and us. It was only marginally encouraging to learn that the ones who remained chose not to kill, but nevertheless, they still preyed on humans. Time would tell.

We stopped in front of a storefront that had been vacant for the last few months. I'd passed it many times, noticing the For Lease sign in the window. It was dark beyond the glass windows, and I stole a peek at Liam's expression before I fished out the keys from my coat pocket.

"What's this?" he asked.

Not answering him right away, I unlocked the door and walked in. Liam followed me. I found the lights and flipped them on. The place was under serious renovation. Construction materials and equipment was everywhere.

Liam looked completely confused, and I enjoyed dragging out the suspense. "What do you think?" I asked, observing his reaction.

Liam looked all around the room, maybe searching for clues. "I don't know. What is this place going to be?" he asked.

I was giddy with excitement and humming with energy. "This is the new Parker Art Studio, featuring the work of yours truly and other fine local artists," I said, nervous excitement spilling from me. I'd been on pins and needles wondering if he would see my vision and hopefully want to stick around to see it grow. It was my first leap of faith. Liam McKenzie was the next if he chose to stay.

He blinked at me several times as my words sunk in. I held my breath. And then slowly a smile spread across his face. "This is your studio?" I nodded enthusiastically. "What about your job?" he asked, but I could tell he liked the idea.

"I put in my resignation letter three days ago," I said, feeling free for the first time in my life. And a little terrified.

"You're kidding." I shook my head, smiling like the cat who just ate the canary.

Liam's face grew animated, and he suddenly picked me up and spun me around. I squealed with delight. I'd been dying to share this with him, but wanted to be sure it was going to work out. Now, if I could convince him to stay, everything would be perfect—minus vampires, and full moons.

Did full moons even influence him? I'd gotten my education about such things from the movies, like every other red-blooded American kid, so I had a lot to learn.

When he stopped spinning me, I felt breathless. Liam leaned down and kissed me. I returned his kiss with all the passion and need I had for this incredible man.

When he finally pulled back, I searched his eyes. "Will you stay? I promise that no matter what happens between us, I'll never share your secret. You can trust me."

"I'm not going anywhere," he said, claiming my lips again.

It was like the final piece of the puzzle fell into place and everything just fit. I felt balanced and finally understood where my life had been leading me. All the dreams, and seemingly wrong turns—which turned out to be part of the journey and not wrong at all—led me to him and a deeper understanding of myself.

That was the happiest moment of my life. I knew, if Liam McKenzie was going to be a part of it, I was bound to have many more, and some of them would be wild.

27

*S*eth
          The Moon was more mellow than usual. Home-
coming week must have taken its toll on everyone. The big
fire on campus may have contributed to that. Cole returned
from the bar carrying four beers. He handed one to each of
the two college girls we were talking to.

Now that Liam and Jess seemed bound at the hip, Cole
and I had to go to work at the station just to get some time
with our older brother. It was cool. Neither of us blamed
him. I was sincerely happy for Liam. He seemed really
content, and that gave me some peace.

It felt good to know that a small handful of people knew
our secret and seemed okay with keeping it. I felt less alone
than I had in a very long time.

The girls laughed loudly at something, and I tried not to
make a face. They were obviously buzzed before they came
over to our table. I wasn't paying attention to what was said,
but I doubted it was that funny.

The blonde was Sandy, or Susan, or something like that.
And the brunette was Bethany. I did manage to remember

that one. Maybe because every time I looked at her, I thought of another brunette I'd recently met.

Olivia would steal into my thoughts more often than I'd ever admitted. My head was usually filled with beautiful women, and I liked it that way. Variety was the spice of life, right?

Bethany was coming on strong. She laughed at everything I said, and it was starting to get annoying. She had cozied up under my free arm so that I had it resting on her shoulders. Her doing, not mine.

She was cute enough and seemed nice enough, but something was off with me. I suddenly found myself being picky.. Every woman I'd met or hung out with over the last few weeks had lost my interest quickly. I still couldn't put my finger on it. Maybe I was losing my touch.

Cole wasn't interested in what's-her-name anyway. He kept glancing over at the bar, and I knew why. He was waiting for Zoey to come on shift. He always insisted we come here whenever I mentioned a different bar. Cole had it bad for Zoey, and learning she was a witch hadn't done a thing to dampen his interest. Maybe it encouraged it.

Now they had something in common. She was like us, in that she was different and kept that fact a secret. "Who are you looking for, Cole?" I teased. Cole turned and gave me a dirty look.

"No one," he said, for the benefit of the girls.

"Do you guys want to take this party to our apartment?" the blonde one asked, gazing at Cole.

"They've got plans that don't include you," a familiar female voice said coolly. The girls jumped.

Olivia stood there staring at me with an amused expression on her face. Cole and I exchanged a look. My friendly younger brother wasn't too crazy about Olivia and her kind sticking around town. I wasn't that happy about the vamps moving in either…except, for Olivia. She intrigued me. There was something about her.

"And what do you know about it?" demanded the brunette.

Olivia got in the girls' face in a most menacing way. "He's with me, so move along, little girl." Bethany looked like she was going to explode. Her face turned red within seconds, and her mouth was moving, but so far no words had come out.

Bethany spun on me. "Is she telling the truth? Is this your girlfriend?" she demanded.

I looked at Olivia who had crossed her arms over her chest and was challenging me with her stare. "I guess so," I said, never looking away from Olivia's gaze.

Bethany huffed and grabbed her jacket from the back of her chair. "Let's go, Susan. These guys are creeps." Both girls turned and marched out of the bar.

"You're welcome," Olivia said, picking up one of the beers the girls had left and taking a long swig.

"For what? How do you know we didn't like those girls? We were just about to go to their apartment," Cole said, sounding indignant.

Olivia sat down in a chair next to me and put her boots up on the table, inviting herself to join us. "No, you weren't. Neither one of you liked those girls, and you have a crush on that one," Olivia said, pointing her beer toward the bar.

We followed her gaze, and there was Zoey, tying on a black apron to start her shift. She glanced up at us with a curious look on her face. Maybe because Olivia was with us.

Zoey smiled weakly and waved. Cole smiled and waved back. And Olivia raised her bottle to her in greeting. Cole turned back to Olivia.

"What do you know about it?" he grumbled.

"I'm good at reading people. Are you going to lie and say you don't?" she asked, raising her eyebrows.

"Mind your own business," Cole said, taking his beer and stalking to the bar.

"He really doesn't like me, does he?" Olivia said, watching Cole walk away.

"He's a little testy where Zoey's concerned," I offered, studying her features while she wasn't looking.

She turned to me. "What about you? Do you like me?"

There was a challenge there, but I wasn't sure what she wanted me to say. "I don't know. I don't really know you, do I?" I asked. I did like her, in spite of myself. There was something compelling about Olivia, and I didn't think it had anything to do with her being a vampire.

"No, you don't," she said.

"Why did you help us find Lorenzo, really?"

An angry expression crossed her face, but she smoothed it away quickly. "Lorenzo was a piece of shit and deserved to die the final death. He was despicable in life and in death," she said, staring off as if lost in memories.

"Does that mean that all vampires are evil, just some more evil than others?" I asked and knew immediately that I'd struck a chord.

She glared at me before breaking eye contact. A few moments passed. "He's dead, you know. Victor said there was no way to survive a bite from one of your kind."

"Good to know. What about my question?" I pressed.

She tossed back the last of her borrowed beer and stood up. She wore a loose white blouse under a navy pea coat, with jeans and cowboy boots. This was a slightly more polished, yet eclectic style in comparison to the college casual I'd seen her wear. She looked older, somehow, and I wondered how long she'd been a vampire and what her actual age was.

She looked down at me, and I couldn't help thinking how beautiful and normal she seemed. Only the specs of iridescent color in her light brown eyes hinted at something else. "You'll have to figure that out on your own," she said, and it was almost a whisper. Then, she walked toward the doors, stopped, and turned back around.

"I almost forgot to tell you why I came." I leaned forward, intent on what she had to say but distracted by her glossy pink lips. "Victor knows something about you and your brothers."

My body tensed. "What does he know?" I asked slowly, trying to control the emotions her words brought.

She shrugged. "I don't know what it is. I just overheard him saying something to Elizabeth about it. They clammed up when I walked into the room." She seemed to take notice of my reaction. "I'll let you know if I learn what it is."

"Thank you," I said, watching her. She smiled a small smile, and it seemed out of character for her tough image. She turned and walked to the door, but looked back one last time. Then she was gone.

A million thoughts ran through my mind. Our birth mother came rushing into my thoughts, almost like a forbidden ghost I'd banned a long time ago.

I'd spent a couple of years hunting down any clue I could find about her, about our past. I'd paid for every internet service I could find to search for information about her, but I always came up empty. I'd even hired a detective who spent over a year searching but hit a dead end.

I finally gave up. She really was a ghost and Liam, Cole, and I was her forgotten inheritance. Now, Olivia may have information I'd have no way of learning.

Fate was a fickle mistress.

Liam and Cole would not like learning that the vampires

could hold the key to our past. We'd been asking ourselves why so long, we finally stopped talking about it.

But it was always there, like an itch that would never go away.

The truth was the only remedy.

the end...

.

Did you enjoy this book?
Consider leaving a review on any major retailer and/or Goodreads. Reviews are the single best way to help new readers discover a good story and an excellent way to support your favorite Indie Authors--so we can continue doing what we love by entertaining readers.

Turn the page to learn about...
IGNITE
BOOK TWO
BURNING MOON SERIES.

BURNING MOON ~ BOOK TWO

Hiding in plain sight was easy...until the vampires came to town.
In a small college town, nestled in the mountains of Arizona, three
firefighting brothers struggle to control and hide their inner beasts;
all while protecting a community who can never know the truth.

Seth McKenzie, the brother with a reputation among the ladies, can't seem to keep his thoughts from Olivia, one of the vampires. When a dangerous past threatens Olivia, Seth discovers that he'll do anything to protect her.

Olivia is the youngest and most rebellious of the vampire clan who've taken up residency in the transient college town. She thought the worst had already happened when she'd had vampirism forced on her years ago—she was wrong. When an unknown enemy catches up with her, Olivia will have to decide whether to cut and run or stay and risk a fate worse than the final death. Especially, if she hopes to protect a certain attractive, yet frustrating, wolf-shifter who makes her feel things she thought she'd never feel again.

Paranormal romantic suspense and urban fantasy

Turn the page for excerpt.

CHAPTER 1

Seth

The music seemed louder than usual at the Burning Moon Bar. Or maybe it was just my mood that made everything, even the small things, seem annoying.

When Cole had asked me to join him for drinks and a few games of darts, I'd considered blowing him off. Staying home and tinkering with my old truck had seemed more appealing.

The following day was Cole's twenty-third birthday, and since our older brother, Liam, spent every spare moment with his girlfriend, Jessica, I didn't feel right about leaving Cole hanging.

"Are you going to throw or what?" Cole asked.

His question snapped my focus back to our game. I usually won when we played darts, but he'd managed to kick my ass two games in a row. This would be the third time tonight he'd beaten me. That hadn't helped to improve my mood.

"Yeah, yeah." I moved into position.

Pulling back the dart, I sent it flying toward the board. It bounced off my other dart and fell to the floor, silently.

"Ha! You buy the next round. I won again." Cole was more energetic than he normally was, and normal for him was what I assumed a squirrel on crack was like.

I shot him an annoyed look before placing the darts in the cup next to the game board so someone else could play. Cole ran his fingers through his short sandy blond hair and studied me a moment. My younger brother's scrutiny made me uncomfortable.

"What's up with you? You haven't seemed like yourself lately," Cole said, dropping his teasing tone for a more serious one. He was shorter and stockier than Liam and me, and he was as solid as a brick wall. You only had to underestimate Cole once to know better.

What was up with me? I'd been out of it for a few weeks now. Even though I knew exactly what he was talking about, I wasn't in the mood to be analyzed by Cole, so I played dumb. "What's that supposed to mean?"

"You're moping around, and you're letting me beat you in darts."

"I didn't *let* you beat me," I said irritably.

"You know what I mean. You're way too serious, and you haven't cracked any bad jokes." Cole eyed me before he took a sip of his beer. He was a cross between a college student and a cowboy, wearing his jeans, western boots, and a belt with a large buckle. His vintage Van Halen T-shirt was probably thrown in to keep you guessing. Cole didn't like to be put in any one box.

"Want to know how I know something's off with you?" He leaned back in his chair with a smug expression.

I rolled my eyes to the ceiling. "I can hardly wait to hear."

"The way I know is you haven't chased a single woman tonight. I don't think you've had a date in almost three weeks —at least that I know of." Cole tossed back the last of his beer, then picked up where he left off. "It's just not like you. What gives?"

I wish I knew.

"I don't know what my problem is. I guess I'm a bit out of sorts, as Ma would have said." I waved my credit card at the bartender to signal that I was ready to close out our tab.

"You can talk to me. I mean, what is family for? Right?" Cole grasped my shoulder with an encouraging smile. I knew his concern was genuine. This wasn't like me and we both knew it.

"It'll pass. Maybe it's an emotional letdown after all the excitement over the rogue vampire Liam put down," I said.

Was I turning into an adrenaline junky after one risky encounter? Aren't most firefighters?

Cole looked thoughtful. "It has been quiet since the fire and kidnapping. I'd hate to be the vampire that stood between Liam and Jessica," Cole said, shaking his head.

I had to agree with him there. Big Brother Liam was in love. He'd found his *true mate*, or rather, fate had thrown them together. I didn't want to imagine Liam if he'd lost Jessica. At times they were hard to be around. Their happiness either made me feel all warm and fuzzy inside or made me want to throw up.

Zoey, the bartender, walked over to take my card. She snatched it out of my hand and left before I could tease her. It was fun to pick on her. Her green eyes flashed from dark to light emerald when she was annoyed.

Cole's gaze followed the attractive redhead as she made her way to the cash register on the other side of the bar.

"When are you going to ask that woman out?" I asked, nudging his shoulder. "What's the worst that could happen?" It was my turn to be the supportive brother, and the new subject took the focus off of me.

He turned a wary gaze my way. "I did. She shot me down, just like I knew she would. Just like she's done every guy in town since she showed up."

"Oh, I see. She's only been here a few months. Give her some time." I squeezed his shoulder once more before I let it drop. I'd assumed Zoey had a soft spot for Cole because she was always friendlier, gentler when dealing with him. Maybe she knew he liked her and felt bad that she didn't feel the same. Women like that were too much work. We'd all be happier when he moved on. I didn't enjoy the idea of seeing him get his heart broken.

Zoey came back with my card and a bill for me to sign.

"You boys heading home for the night or looking for the next party?" Zoey asked Cole.

He perked up and smiled at her. "Heading home. I'm pretty exhausted after kicking Seth's butt in darts four times."

"Three," I corrected.

Zoey turned her intense gaze on me. "Is that so? What's up with you, Seth? Not like you to let anyone beat you. And no barflies to take home? It's a sad night for the middle child in the McKenzie family."

She wasn't usually so talkative. Cole was riveted by the attention she was showing us. I feigned a hurt look and put a hand over my heart.

"Tomorrow's your birthday, right, Cole?" Zoey asked as we turned to leave. Cole looked surprised that she mentioned it.

"Yeah, how'd you know?" he asked.

She smiled at him. "A little bird told me. Can I be the first to wish you an early happy birthday?"

Cole nodded and watched as she turned away and began taking other orders. He turned to me as though he were in a daze. I swung him in the direction of the door and pushed him through the crowd. When we stepped outside, the chilled night air was a welcome relief from the stuffy bar.

Cole had been crushing on Zoey since the first day he'd laid eyes on her, but she didn't seem interested in dating anyone. She shot me down the first week. I'd made it a game after that, but she never took me seriously and didn't seem affected by my charms—many of which I was damned proud of. Sometimes I flirted with her just to bug Cole. Tonight was different. I thought she may have been flirting with Cole, whether she knew it or not.

"Don't give up on her so easily," I said as warmly dressed people passed us on their way to restaurants or bars. The historic downtown area of Flagstaff was always busy, especially the nightlife.

"Why do you say that?" Cole asked.

The sidewalks deserted as we turned down a quieter street and made our way to Cole's hard-topped Jeep.

"I have a feeling about Zoey. It sure seems like she likes you. At least she likes you better than me," I said, giving him a sideways grin.

When we'd learned that Zoey was a witch, the idea hadn't dampened the flames of Cole's attraction toward her. I believed it had solidified it. Zoey was the first person we'd met in a very long time who had to hide her true nature from the world, just as we hid our inner wolf.

"I don't know. Do you think she's gay? I mean, she turns down every guy that asks her out. Maybe I'm barking up the wrong tree," Cole said. The alleyway where Cole had parked that night was dimly lit.

"I don't think that's the . . ."

Someone was in the shadows—two someones. It wasn't the form of two people making out against the brick wall that made us stop abruptly. *It was the smell of blood.*

There was another smell that made my nostrils flare and

caused my wolf to stir. Cole growled low in his chest.

Vampire.

As my vision adjusted to the dark alley, I could see a male figure peel away from a woman to step into the sparsely lit alley. He had blood on his lips. The woman moaned but stayed where she was. I had the feeling her sound had nothing to do with fear and everything to do with pleasure, but Cole must not have had the same vibe.

"Get away from her," Cole ordered, his voice sounding like he had too many teeth in his mouth.

The vampire watched us like he was waiting to see what we'd do. "You're upsetting my date," he said, making no move to leave or flee.

I put a hand on Cole's shoulder to calm him. It was a wolf thing—a touch from a pack member had a way of relaxing the other, allowing them to get their wolf under control.

"Your date or your meal?" I asked coolly.

"Why is it any of your business?" The vampire took a bold step toward us.

The man had sandy-blonde hair, like Cole's, and a goatee. He was tall, well-built, and looked like any other human we'd passed on the street that night. The only giveaway was his iridescent blue eyes that grew lighter as his emotions seemed to intensify. I'd noticed the same response with Olivia's eyes. "This is our town, our community, and our friends. When you hurt one of them, we take it personally," I said, stepping closer but motioning for Cole to stay back.

The woman moaned again. The vampire glanced over toward her, a mocking smile on his bloody lips. "Be right there, love." He turned his attention back to Cole and me. "As you can see, she's perfectly happy. No harm has come to her and none will. You need to be on your way, little wolves."

I bristled at his taunt but wasn't about to let it show. He was obviously ready for a fight, which may have meant he wasn't alone. We needed to walk away from this one and figure out what to do about the vampires in the light of day and with a clear head.

Olivia had assured me that vampires didn't need to kill to survive, and the victims had no memories of what had happened when it was handled properly. Lorenzo had been an exception, according to her. I hoped she was telling me the truth.

"I need to know for certain," I said, staring down the vampire.

He glared at me for a few moments, then walked back to the woman and led her gently into the light. She clung to him as if in adoration.

"Lesley, my love, tell this man how many dates we've had so he will leave us in peace." The vampire stroked the woman's arm affectionately.

She had the grace to look embarrassed. "This is our fourth date. I'm perfectly safe with Edgar, I can assure you," she said, leaning her head against his chest.

Bite marks on her neck were obvious, but she didn't look unusually pale or in any immediate danger. Still, I wasn't certain how this situation was going to play out with the vampires. I didn't see how we could all live in the same town.

I tried to walk cautiously past Edgar and Lesley, attempting to pull Cole along with me until he dug his heels in and stopped us both.

"What are you doing, Seth? We can't leave her with that thing." Cole jerked his arm out of my grasp.

"She's fine, Cole. Let's go."

Cole glared at me as if I'd just betrayed some sacred oath. He glared at the vampire as he stalked toward his Jeep, parked at the other end of the alley.

I watched him get into the Jeep, then turned to look back one more time, but the vampire and the woman were gone. I wondered if I'd made the right decision as I walked toward the Jeep. I knew that in Cole's eyes I hadn't lived up to his expectations, at least where the vampires were concerned.

CHAPTER 2

The situation with the vampire had been on my mind all day. Cole had barely said two words to me before he'd dropped me off at my apartment, which was located above an auto repair shop.

It was Cole's birthday, and we were having a barbecue at Liam's property. My older brother's log-cabin home wouldn't be complete for a few more months, so we decided to work the grill and make a bonfire to keep the ladies warm.

Feeling like I needed to do something to snap myself out of the rut I'd been in, I'd invited Marissa, a nurse I sometimes dated, to Cole's small party. She knew we were casual and didn't seem to mind being my date now and again. There was no pressure with Marissa, and I liked that.

Marissa and I arrived early to help Liam and Jessica set up. We had about an hour before the sun began to set. Jessica had insisted on helium balloons be tied to the folding chairs or anyplace that I could find to attach them. Several had already popped, and each time one did, Jess gave me a look that said she wished she'd given the job to someone else.

After the third balloon popped, Marissa took the

remaining four balloons out of my hands. "Go see if Liam needs help with the bonfire."

"Fine by me," I said, relieved.

It was nice having Jessica around. Liam was certainly more relaxed these days. I hadn't seen him this way in a long time—maybe since we were kids. At a young age, he became responsible for Cole and me, and it changed him from happy-go-lucky to cool and cautious. Gone was the youthful lighthearted nature that had made him so popular through high school.

Liam had just finished stacking enough wood to keep the fire going for days. He was staring contently into the blaze when I walked over. "Nice job."

"Thanks," he said.

Daisy, Jessica's best friend, walked up to me and put a bowl of potato salad in my arms. "Make yourself useful, Seth. Put that on the table and find the paper plates."

"I suddenly know what's wrong here. There's too much estrogen in the air. Women just love to boss men around," I said, depositing the bowl on the folding table covered in a clean red-and-white checkered tablecloth.

Since when did we use a tablecloth? When had Liam ever owned a tablecloth for that matter?

Cole's Jeep could be heard before it was seen coming down the long gravel drive—a cloud of dust floated behind him. He parked and climbed out carrying a grocery bag and wearing a cheesy grin.

I was glad to see he was in good humor. After the situation with the vampire the night before, I was worried he'd still be angry with me. Cole didn't hold a grudge, but he did have a temper. He walked up to Liam and gave him a rough hug.

"Happy birthday, Cole," Liam said, taking the grocery bag from him.

"Thanks, Liam. I picked up some more beer." He ran his hand through his hair, then walked over to me. I met him halfway and wrapped him in a brotherly embrace. Cole held on a little longer than normal.

When he finally pulled away, I asked, "We good?"

He smiled his boyish grin and nodded.

"Cole!" Jessica yelled excitedly. She hurried from the fifth-wheel trailer that Liam used as a temporary home while the cabin was under construction.

Cole hugged Jessica and spun her around. "I have your favorite cake—chocolate with buttercream frosting," Jess said happily.

"Okay, but that's not my favorite cake," Cole said.

Jessica looked confused. She turned around toward Liam, her hands on her hips. "I thought you said that was his favorite?"

Liam smiled slyly. "You must have misunderstood. I said chocolate cake with buttercream frosting was my favorite."

Cole and I laughed hard. When I had it under control, I said, "It's okay, Jessica. It's an old family joke. It happens every year, at every birthday."

Cole was grinning and shaking his head, but Jessica didn't seem to appreciate the joke or Liam.

"Well, I don't see the humor, myself," Jessica said before walking away.

"Maybe time to change that tradition, Liam. I think you're in the doghouse now," I said, as Cole and I began cracking up all over again.

"She'll get used to our ways, just like I'm getting used to hers." He smiled and lifted a corner of the plaid tablecloth. "The grill is hot. Let's start cooking."

Nothing could beat an Arizona sunset for its spectacular beauty. Red, orange, pink, and purple smeared across the sky like a neon watercolor painting.

Daisy's date arrived, just after sunset. His name was Eric, and he worked at the morgue. They stood close and occasionally held hands but didn't seem totally together. Maybe it was more like Marissa and me—friends with occasional benefits.

Marissa knew everyone there, so she had no trouble making herself useful and chatting with whoever was near. Jessica had the side dishes and condiments neatly arranged while Liam worked the grill, cooking hamburgers and hot dogs. Daisy had insisted on chicken and provided her own chicken breast for Liam to grill. She didn't eat red meat, a thought I couldn't comprehend.

We were just about to start eating when someone on a motorcycle came down the driveway. It was a smaller bike than mine, but I was still surprised to realize a woman was driving it.

Snug jeans and a sheepskin-collared leather jacket gave away the curves that were undeniably feminine. When she pulled off the shiny black helmet, I was equally surprised to recognize Zoey as she climbed off the bike.

I looked over at Cole to see his mouth hanging open and his eyes wide. He immediately walked over to her. When she had rested her helmet on the handlebars, she shook her long red hair out and smiled at Cole. "Happy birthday, handsome. Sorry if I'm late. The bar was packed, and I had a hard time convincing my boss to let me leave." She hugged Cole and kissed his cheek briefly.

"How'd you know there was a party? I mean, I'm happy you're here, but how did you . . ." Cole said, stumbling over his words.

"I invited her," I said.

She gave me a quick hug but no kiss, I noticed. I guessed those were reserved for birthdays. I didn't think she'd show, but I'd thought it was worth a shot.

"So did I!" Jessica brushed past me to welcome Zoey herself.

Cole stared at me like he didn't know if he should thank me or kick my ass. I winked at him and put my arm around Marissa.

"Thanks for coming. I would have invited you, but didn't think you'd want to come," Cole said.

"Why wouldn't I?" she asked, moving past Cole and closer to the fire. She smiled as she greeted the others.

Cole followed her. "Well, you turned me down for a date, and I thought . . ."

She smiled at him, and his face glazed over like it had when she'd spoken to him last night. "It's your birthday, Cole. Lighten up."

After the initial shock wore off, Cole seemed happy to have Zoey at his birthday celebration. I knew he would be. It was a last-minute decision on my part, but it made sense that she should be there with us. After all, she kept our greatest secret and we kept hers.

The bonfire raged, the smell of smoke and pine was heavy in the air, and the stars twinkled in the night sky. Liam's land was surrounded by national forests on three sides and the highway on the other. We'd all eaten our fill and were huddled around the fire sharing funny stories. The mood was light and festive, but I couldn't help feeling restless. It was like there was something missing for me.

I caught her scent before I saw her small dark form separate from the forest and begin to walk toward us. It was as if she was summoned from my mind. Olivia and her constant shadow, Simon, walked at an ordinary pace—maybe for the humans in our midst. At least two people there didn't share our secret, Daisy's date and mine.

I felt the tension rolling off Cole and Liam. Liam moved in front of Jessica, and Cole took several steps toward the uninvited guests. "Easy, Cole," I said cautiously.

"Did you invite them?" Cole demanded.

"No, but let me handle this." I walked out to meet the two vampires before they reached our group.

"What's going on?" I heard Marissa ask.

Olivia's long brown hair was blowing in the breeze as she walked toward me. Her jeans were shredded, in the popular style, and not nearly warm enough for this weather. I knew the temperature didn't matter to her. At least she was wearing an oversized leather jacket, even if it looked like it might have been a man's.

Olivia intrigued me like no other woman ever had, and that fact was starting to bug the hell out of me.

I stopped and let them meet me in the middle of the field. A slight smile played at her lips, making my gut tighten in response. *What was Olivia up to?*

"Olivia. Simon." I crossed my arms and watched them warily.

Olivia stopped in front of me and glanced over my shoulder at the others gathered around the fire. "A party? And you didn't invite me? I think I'm hurt."

She didn't sound hurt, but I suddenly felt guilty for not inviting her. She had that sort of effect on me—always knocking me off my game.

"It's a birthday party for Cole, and you are not his favorite person—or species for that matter," I said.

I didn't want to hurt her, but this was new territory for us and her intentions were unclear.

"I don't have anything against Cole, even if he's a bit hotheaded. Do you, Simon?" Olivia asked over her shoulder.

Simon, a young looking Jamaican man with long dread-locks, wore a leather baseball jacket from a high school that I didn't recognize. He didn't bother to reply. His expression-less face just watched me, as if bored. I'd always had the feeling that it would be a mistake to underestimate the quiet shadow that followed Olivia.

I wondered what their relationship was. Thinking of them as lovers made me angry, but I tried not to let it show.

"You should probably leave. I don't want to spoil Cole's birthday if your presence will cause tension," I said as gently as I could.

She looked past me again. "They're discussing it now. Sounds like the blonde thinks you should invite us to stay a while. What do you think, Seth?" she asked, her tone chal-lenging.

I wasn't certain what Olivia wanted from me and didn't understand my feelings toward her. I felt conflicted when I thought about her, which was more often than I cared to admit.

"You can hear them?" I asked, surprised.

"Yes, my hearing is better than a shifter's," she said while appearing to focus on a conversation I couldn't discern.

I looked over my shoulder to see Cole, Liam, and Jessica in what looked like a serious discussion. They all looked our way before Liam began walking toward us.

"They decided to invite us to stay a while," Olivia said with a smug smile. She stared at me with a defiantly gleam in her eyes. I didn't know if I wanted to kiss her or turn her over my knee and spank her.

Liam reached us and looked critically at the two vampires. "We have two friends that don't know what we are and don't know about vampires, so if you two can behave yourselves, we'd like to invite you to join us."

Olivia smiled at Liam before looking at Simon. Simon

nodded and began walking toward the fire without any hesitation.

"Thank you. We'd love to join you," Olivia said, giving me a sideways glance before following Simon.

Liam looked at me. "Do they mean trouble?"

"I don't think so. I get the feeling Olivia's lonely. It doesn't seem like she gets along with her people very well," I said as we turned to follow them back to the fire.

"Except Simon. What's the story with them? Are they together?" Liam asked.

"I have no clue. I'm no expert on vampires, and she's more confusing than the rest of them."

Liam nodded, and I heard Olivia's soft laughter. This would be an interesting evening--anything could happen.

Vampires were coming to a shifter party.

IGNITE ~ BOOK TWO

https://www.rkclosebooks.com/ignite

THE VAMPIRE FILES

★★★★★ **Oh yes, please!**

"I'm an enthusiastic vampire fan, though I haven't read much

of it since Twilight. This book reminds me that I'VE BEEN
MISSING OUT!!! Fast-paced, funny, with a sassy main
character and swoon-worthy bad boys, I loved everything
about Red Night." **Reader Review**

LEARN MORE AT
https://www.rkclosebooks.com/red-night
OR
RKCLOSEBOOKS.COM

AUTHOR NOTE

At the time of publication, I was attending an author conference in Las Vegas. For an introvert, a conference of any scale can be challenging, but I was proud that I didn't hide in my hotel room. *Okay, I ordered in one night.*

I had the pleasure of meeting and hanging out with many wonderful authors in various stages of the writing journey. This particular conference was for Indie and Hybrid Authors.

After several years, I finally had the pleasure of meeting Lucy, a longtime internet friend, and a couple of other acquaintances (Monique and Tracy) from one of my favorite online author groups, Love Kissed. Somehow, the three lovely authors that I teamed up with were all from Australia. They made the conference fun and more enjoyable. If these three are any reflection, Australian's are fun-loving, warm-hearted, and possess a great sense of humor. They kept me laughing all week.

Spark is the fifth release for me and I'm incredibly grateful to still be on this incredible path. Like many of you, life has been busy. Between losing my mind to meet the deadlines for this book, oldest daughter moving out, our son graduating high school and starting college, the demands of high school for our youngest who doesn't drive herself yet (did I say author—I meant taxi driver, maid, cook, and laundry service), husband ready for retirement, aging parents, book deadlines, holidays sneaking up on me, and a house full of needy pets, I'm ready for a vacation. Unfortunately, I don't have any exciting trips to tell you about. Maybe by the next book. *wink, wink*

Happy Reading.

R.K. Close

ABOUT THE AUTHOR

Best selling Author, R.K. Close blends urban fantasy and paranormal romantic suspense into fast-paced, hard-to-put-down, supernatural adventures that keep fans coming back for more.

This Author began writing for Limitless Publishing when she released the Vampire Files trilogy and now publishes series like the Burning Moon under her own Indie label. Her series takes place in various cities or towns in her home state of Arizona where she's had many adventures of her own.

An outdoor enthusiast, nomadic traveler, wife, mother, and lover of all things curry, R.K. spends her spare time with her head in a book, behind a camera or walking her three high-maintenance dogs. Her book addiction began in high school and bloomed into a writing career later in life.

Never miss a new release, giveaway, sale or freebie. Subscribe to R.K. Close's Books With Bite newsletter today!

https://www.subscribepage.com/Spark_Burning_Moon

WHERE DO YOU HANG OUT?

Follow and connect with RK CLOSE.
Facebook
https://www.facebook.com/rkclose/
BookBub
https://www.bookbub.com/authors/rk-close
Twitter
https://twitter.com/RKClose_Tweets
Website
http://www.rkclosebooks.com/
Goodreads
http://www.goodreads.com/RKClose
Instagram
https://www.instagram.com/rkclose/
Books with Bite
Newsletter
https://www.subscribepage.com/Ignite_Subscribe
Email
RKClose@RKCloseBooks.com

ACKNOWLEDGEMENTS

There are so many people in my life that support me in this journey. I wish to mention a few in each book. I'd like to thank God for my salvation and His grace. A big thank you to the man behind this woman, my husband, Greg, who loves me for who I am and encourages me to work toward my dreams. My children have supported and tolerated my writing at the expense of meals and sometimes clean clothing. I could not and would not do this without their love and support--my family is my joy and they inspire me to strive to be the best I can be.

My parents have always been my cheerleaders and I'm eternally grateful that God chose to bless me with their unwavering love and guidance in my life--even if they don't read my book. ;)

Of course, for all the many Indie Authors who've helped teach and inspire me along my journey--I salute you. I know how hard you work for the words and the readers. The Indie Author community is incredibly generous and nurturing.

And, my greatest thank you goes to you, the reader. Without you, it's only words on a page.

Made in the USA
Columbia, SC
29 January 2020